Remembering
CARMEN

Remembering
CARMEN

~ Nicholas Murray ~

seren

Seren is the book imprint of
Poetry Wales Press Ltd
Nolton Street, Bridgend, CF31 3BN, Wales
www.seren-books.com

© Nicholas Murray, 2003

ISBN 1-85411-337-2

A CIP record for this title is available from
the British Library

*The publisher works with the financial assistance of the
Welsh Books Council*

Printed in Plantin by CPD (Wales), Ebbw Vale

~ ONE ~

Deftly, like an actress who has practised her moves in a clattering morning rehearsal room, the latest one slips from his bed, trailing her nakedness in her wake.

Seconds later, he hears the rush of water from the shower, imagines her in the steam, foresees the inexorable steps in the grooming sequence, traces in anticipation the rapid smile – perhaps even the concession of a rapid kiss – and then the swift, accurately paced departure. The door's click. The footfall on the stair. The consequent silence.

In this way he has passed the weeks, the months, since Carmen.

It may be that love comes once and once only, preceded by rehearsal, followed by regret. How snugly, thinks Christopher, I fit into this oh-too-neat paradigm. The years before Carmen were unsettled and unsatisfactory. Since her departure, since the onset of her absence, he has felt himself to be living in the aftermath of his own life, an odd survivor in the interstices of old routine. She has been the ghost flitting unnoticed in the background of these casual, unconsidered intimacies. She has left her legacy which he measures out like an old skinflint, hoping that the diminished remnant will outlast him as a symbolic residue – nugatory, almost weightless – to be turned over admiringly when he is gone.

Carmen, he says, this is what you have done to me: made me your reluctant memorialist. What happened to our reckless disregard for time and place? At what point did we abandon our exalted indifference?

~

A clear recollection: the terrace of a white hotel facing the sea. He cannot escape the compulsion to begin at the beginning. But is this the beginning? They quarrelled, even about this.

They sit (in Christopher's disputed version) in separate chairs, facing a low wall in whose cavity is planted an aromatic hedge. On the table in front of his cane seat (upholstered with loose calico cushions) a basket rests on the white linen cloth. Wrapped in a soft napkin are a warm bread roll, a flaky croissant. He mixes a cup of strong coffee with boiled milk from a plump little jug. He hacks unsuccessfully at one of the rectangular lozenges of butter which slides about in a flat dish, its hardness assured by two tiny cubes of ice. He knows now that she will have been waiting, calmly, for the sun to soften her ration. She will have been less inept than he at spooning apricot preserve on to the exposed fibre of a torn croissant. The crisp linen will not have been soiled with a variety of clumsy stains.

It is important to establish which of them spoke first. "Typical male," was her response to his proposal – in the course of their later dissection of this contested scene – that he had been the first to break the morning silence with some vacuous pleasantry. Their tables are identical. Christopher has brought only a key attached to a heavy brass ball. Carmen is unfolding the new day's *Le Monde*. Perhaps he says something like this (in English, which from an overheard prior interchange with the waiter, he has established to be her native language):

"Let's hope we've seen the last of the rain."

Christopher gestures to the glorious brightness of the morning sun, which glows with promise in a rinsed, blue sky. He calls on it with the uncertain aplomb of a barrister summoning a witness in whom he has no confidence. Carmen is wearing dark sunglasses which she chooses not to remove. She turns in his direction, saying nothing at first. It is as if she is trying to establish whether such a banal reflection merits the effort of a reply. Then she removes her glasses, placing them in the hollow of the newspaper in her lap. Christopher thinks that much of their subsequent career together is predicated in that brief exchange.

"That's certainly how it looks."

Perhaps, even then, he had misgivings, sensing in her tone a sort of sly mockery, an exquisitely refined contempt. But these falterings do not last. He looks at her carefully, struck by the way in which she holds herself, proudly, confident of her ungainsayable beauty, but without arrogance. She balances the consciousness that she has the power to turn heads with an easy carelessness. That is what he comes to love in her: her gift of prodigality. She has more than this to spare. She lacks his desperate habit of trying always to conjure the most from the least. His ambition. Her skin is pale, in contrast to the tanned skin all around her, and her short black hair (which reminds him of an old-fashioned photograph of Mary Quant) is neatly sculpted. She wears a simple but almost certainly expensive white dress which exposes her slender arms. Everything about her suggests immaculate grooming and perfect self-control. By contrast, he feels himself to be a dishevelled Bohemian, an English lout on the Mediterranean coast. She is pleased, in retrospect, when he uses this formulation in conversation with her.

Later, he produces a photograph. Intended to clinch the matter (the prosecuting barrister's humour restored) the strategy backfires. Christopher has been the photographer, and therefore he is not present in the scene. But the picture is of her and the snap is in his possession. No further questions. But there turn out to be further questions from Carmen. She fires them off, languidly (they are to do with certain unrecognised details on the terrace, a preposterous and intrusive terracotta pot with swathes of embossed vineleaves, certain minor implausibilities in the *mise en scène*) but when he tries to respond she waves a hand. She is bored. It is easier to agree with him. Perhaps then he will go away.

He now thinks: I stayed, Carmen. I stayed. It was you who would leave, in your own good time.

Christopher wonders if his rival was there all the time, like the swirl of ectoplasm in a sepia photograph of an Edwardian seance, flourished in evidence of the existence of the paranormal. A blur of movement. A presence. Not much of a conversationalist, the ineffable Jimmy, his affable monica suggestive of camaraderie, ribbed white sailor's jerseys in the fug of the saloon bar, the clink and slam of dimpled pint pots. The ear-splitting bellow of the male guffaw. Christopher is of the opinion now that she was always disposed to these manly men. She looked on them with contempt but they seemed to satisfy some need in her. A need to mock. She loved to watch their antics. Their vanity played straight into her hands.

Christopher thinks: I am portraying a calculating bitch, a smirking ice-maiden with savage, glittering eyes of cold sapphire, but you were none of these, my love. My Absence. You had everything that I had ever wanted and more. When you opened out there was nothing you could not give. Your generosity had the power to terrify me. With what could I match it? In what coin could I ever repay you? But you did not reduce me. You never did that. I was strong in your strength. We were a partnership, you and I. We were an 'item' – the word we whooped to in a hotel bar in Lincolnshire, leaving its perpetrator (a lank local estate agent) tapping his car-keys on the counter as if they held the open sesame to this cave of laughter from which he was barred.

Could that figure in the photograph have been Jimmy, in disguise? Wrapped in the white togs of an expensive waiter, smarmy and belated, capturing crumbs with a folded napkin, whisking off the detritus of *petit déjeuner*, setting up the goods for the next round of sluggards who had emerged blinking on to the terrace like nocturnal animals rudely disturbed? Unlikely. He was no prankster. He moved lumberingly, like an elephant approaching its stack of logs in a forest clearing, confident that his usual assets – the set of attributes known to teen magazine editors as 'hunk', the sleepy, come-sleep-with-me blue eyes, the blond mop, the delicious languor that waits for insect food to drop unasked into its brimming pool – would see him through. They had always done so in the past.

Christopher thinks now that Jimmy was pre-ordained. Perhaps he had been standing there, just beyond the white margin of the photographic print, all the time. They had simply not noticed. It was his job to call time, to step out of the shadows and say enough is enough. You have had your time in the sun. All debts must be paid. The party is over.

But Christopher reflects: it is not over, Carmen. I am not over you.

~

Carmen considers that her father is to blame. He was a skilled electrician with a taste for collecting playing cards and for light opera. He built himself a plywood bunker along one wall of the living room in which were stacked the vinyl discs of his collection. As children, Carmen and her siblings ran their cars along, or (she was a conventional girl) brought their dolls to interrogate, the white painted plinth on which this intimidating rack of potential sound was raised. The rippled moulding, thickly coated with white gloss paint, sank into the plum-coloured carpet like an abandoned monument sunk in the circumambient sand. Sometimes, when she returned with her mother from exhausting Saturday afternoon assaults on the city department stores, they would open the front door to a wall of sound – a high soprano warbling out her synthetic passion – at a time when other men would be tense before the football game, a light alloy cylinder of weak lager crunched in their excited fist. This spectacle drove her – later – towards the most rebarbative versions of the twentieth century avant-garde string quartet.

And so it was, that the pink, dribbling thing was held up, stowed away to await the arrival of its father (who was lighting a vast industrial chicken shed in East Lancashire), at which moment it was produced by the plump nuns, swathed in folds of white linen. "Carmen!" he called down the echoing corridors of the nursing home. And that was that. That was her christening. Carmen's mother, as in all things, acquiesced.

Later, she was passed into the care of another branch of the peak-bonneted sisterhood who taught her to trill, once a year: "A happy, holy, feast-day, Reverend Mother." Then she left, gladly, their pious groves, read philosophy, fell in with bad company, which was good for her, went off the rails (briefly) and was rescued by a man who was far too old but whose money she took a relish in spending, sometimes with his consent. Foolishly allowing the word "marriage" to slip from the corner of his mouth during one particularly vivid drinking-session, he lost her for good. She came to London where she prospered as a journalist in the young women's magazine sector. She had a knack for delivering what the loose-spending *midinette* wanted to read, two weeks after she should have realised that she did not. When a mild feminism was permissible, she did mild feminism. When feminism went out, at the turn of the century, it went out of her copy. She was quick, adaptable, and delivered the goods. It didn't matter what the goods were as long as they were the goods and were wanted at the time of writing. Carmen was less successful – speaking now of her private life – in those areas about which the magazine – and its star contributor – regularly gave out advice, stricture, encouragement, viz. Relationships. Indeed she was lousy. So inept that one morning she clicked on a cheap-airline website and booked herself a week (longer vacations by this time of the new, enlightened century were frowned upon) to Quelquepart-sur-Mer. On her own. One morning at breakfast some idiot started talking to her about the weather.

~

They had nothing in common. Christopher came to think that this was the secret of their eventual success. Had they been perfectly compatible they should soon have grown bored. Instead they had leisure to discover their dissonances, their gaps, the rich raw material of their quarrels. After that meeting on the terrace (it was his last morning, her first) they both assumed that they would never see each other again. But he met her, four weeks later, in the restaurant queue at the National Film Theatre. She was holding up her tray to receive a plate of mottled quiche and a tumbler of chilled carrot juice. He was bidding for the steak-and-kidney pie. She looked down at his tray with a glance of exhausted compassion. They both spoke at once, which allowed them to laugh, releasing the pressure which had built up unbearably. They shared a table where

Christopher did most of the talking. Carmen would spear another fragment of that sickly quiche, hold it on the tip of her cream-coloured plastic fork, as if daring it to confront those perfect white teeth, then look at him with the languid, resentful detachment of someone who now considers it a mistake to have agreed to visit the zoo. He watched her gestures intently while he babbled. Eventually, she agreed to speak, to give the most economical account possible of her subsequent stay at the Hotel Magnifique. She was tactful enough to avoid all allusion to handsome Jimmy. In truth, he never established – after much forensic activity – whether he had been anything more than a disconnected presence in her life in the course of that week.

It turned out that they had chosen the same film – *Jules et Jim* in black and white (Christopher was always touched by the fate of poor, downcast Jules). Fully recovered now from her disgust at his carniverous eating-habits, she made no protest as he steered her towards the theatre. Afterwards, there was a drink in the bar, some genuinely shared pleasure at dissecting the shortcomings as well as the triumphs of the movie, and then – to the surprise of both – an unforced exchange of addresses.

Naturally, Christopher was the first to phone. Her voice was muffled, as if she were struggling in a dark cupboard or had become engulfed in the folds of a resistant duvet. He could not even be sure it was her. Then the sound clarified (the *pain au chocolat* now swallowed) and she became coherent. Yes, she would be interested in the movie (the new Turkish cinema season: a bold move, he congratulated himself). It turned out to be a little grim: harassment from the authorities down by the Bosphorus, low-budget pain. He had begun to regret not going for something elegantly French at the Renoir.

And so it was that London became the theatre of their

operations. Christopher had recently returned from the country where, for the past seven years, he had earned his living restoring old houses: stone cottages eased out of the hands of the peasantry and sold to the gentlefolk from West Ealing, their windows lovingly 'restored' – with about as much authenticity as would have been provided by an off-the-peg frame from the out-of-town building supply yard, but, pleasantly for him, at four times the cost. He had gradually fallen out of love with his clients, their insufferable pedantry about things of which they knew nothing (mortars, oils, varieties of timber), their inextinguishable self-regard, their air of almost militant self-satisfaction. A series of lucky chances, an unexpected inheritance, had led him to acquire a part-share in a former newsagent's shop in Whitfield Street. His business partner converted the shop (with Christopher's labour) into an organic bean-dispensary and the latter took the upper floor, above his partner's store-room, as his Fitzrovian penthouse. Carmen always referred to it as "Charlotte Street", thinking to wash it in some of the glamour accruing from the presence of the headquarters of Channel 4 Television, several streets away. Christopher's topographical pedantry led him to use the term "Goodge Street" – only the cabbies managing to hear "Whitfield Street" without a "Where's that?" He had always been fond of this part of London and his love now began to deepen. Never again did he wish to see another country-crafts emporium brimming with over-priced ceramics and drippy landscapes painted on warped board. Nor did he wish to look again on the bourgeois weekenders who hogged the pavements of the little market towns, straw baskets affectedly crooked in their arms, enviously measuring the rise of house prices in the windows of wily and smooth-tongued estate agents (the warm rustic burr another weapon in the latter's traditional armoury of deceit). No, Christopher was now a metropolitan, a prickly and polemical 'townie', lodged in his city pad, loving the sheer variousness of its pleasures and practical comforts. Let the red-faced swine gallop across fields on fat-arsed mares in pursuit of the fox! The rest of the civilised world would get on with its proper business. A pox on the 'country folk'!

And, Christopher now reflects: I was in love. You will, will you not, Carmen, concede that?

~

Carmen too reflects: that it began, she supposed, with various visits to the cinema. An accidental meeting was followed by several more undemanding trips to the obvious cultural watering holes. Her frenzied life on the magazine, her pumping out of a glittering stream of bright, worthless words, had destroyed, she now considered, the life of her mind, her ambition (marked by a stiffly bound thesis on ethics presented to a lascivious tutor for the degree of M.Phil, its blue cover and gilt lettering still protected in a polythene bag from the depredations of dust) to write a book which would throw an exciting bridge between the world of the academic specialist and that of the general reader. She considered that she had ruined herself as a thinker, as a user of exact language. Christopher would be furious when she spoke in this way. He saw it as a self-indulgence, a posture. They quarrelled. That was something they were always good at. They knew how to make a vivid argument. Sometimes they were forced to leave a restaurant or a public place because of that vehemence, the sheer visceral violence of their contention. Christopher reflects: Yes, I do miss it. I miss the need and the energy. The compulsion to lock horns and to push against the other's resistance.

When Carmen met Christopher she was resigned to culture as diversion for the exhausted classes. She spent more time in restaurants than in art galleries. The four hour Lear, the dense classic novel, yielded to short movies, light-weight novels, the frothy and the fashionable, the nibbled aesthetic canapé. She was awash with money but denuded of time. Or so it seemed to her at that time. In retrospect she sees that it might not truly have been like this. She could have contended, used some of her famed aggressive-ness against herself. Instead, she preferred to lash out, to make a scene. She is still not sure whether he objected to this. She thinks that they both took pleasure in their endless guerilla campaign against each other. Carmen would come to feel the lack of all that passionate enmity.

Carmen's decision to live with Christopher was in some sense not a decision at all. It simply became, slowly, a reality. Although those first encounters quickly became sexual – for they were, for all their linguistic pugilism and mutual provocations, always attracted to each other, always adroit in their love-making, always ardent – the notion of co-habitation at first revolted them. Neither had been in a recent relationship, neither was recoiling from a failed part-nership or seeking compensatory affairs. They were enjoying the experience of emotional freedom. Christopher had severed his relationship with a life in the sticks about which he refused to talk to Carmen and she was celebrat-ing a narrow escape from matrimony at the hands of an older man. It was precisely this sense of freedom, of light-ness, that attracted them to each other. Carmen considers that she sees this more clearly now than she would have seen it at the time. And there may have been something in Christopher's view that their love of discord, their glorious hostility, was a way of ensuring that each remained free. Like brawling lions, they defended their territory in the simplest possible way, by opening their jaws and letting out a roar.

Notwithstanding their propensity to fight, they grew to need each other. It began with an overnight stay, then a weekend which gradually lengthened at both ends, then an entire week connecting those hitherto separated points. Carmen kept on her flat, of course – a bolt-hole was vital – and Christopher's Whitfield Street lair was large enough to give her a small cubby-hole of her own where she could write while he was out doing his fancy restaurant-fitting. It was a time when her magazine copy was full of references to giving people 'space'. Carmen always thought it would be useful to have throwaway function keys on the lap-top which would cover these set phrases. Most lasted only a year or so, though she was always fascinated by the durability of certain words, their refusal to lie down. The most remarkable of all was 'cool' which strictly speaking should have gone out with leather elbow patches on tweed jackets but which was once again enjoying a revival. It would have to be a permanent function-key.

One thing about which they never quarrelled was London itself. They were both provincials, which she supposed explained their passion for the city – its special freedoms and anonymities, its offer of escape and of choice, the generous permission it grants to various ways of living – the antithesis of the small-town's insistence on its unique path. This large liberty can co-exist with small fixities, routines, grooves. Even in their corner of Fitzrovia they knew their Asian corner-shopman, his wry sense of humour, his predictable jokes, and those of his equally sardonic wife. There was a café – one of the few not yet refitted and homogenised by the big coffee chains – whose furniture was untouched by fashion. It was run by Italians and there was a picture of the Madonna behind the counter.

They had their favourite pubs and restaurants and public places. They walked their own path through the city. They became expert at threading the narrow pavements, dodging people and traffic, discovering the short cuts, the quick back ways that avoided the press of pedestrians on the main thoroughfares. They loved it in the way the countryman, Carmen supposed (unlike Christopher she had never lived in the country and had no desire to do so) loves his fields and hills and the backdrop of sky. She had a passion for travel but always loved to return. It is true that there were parts of the city that seemed alien to her: the great wide streets, parks, mansions and institutions of South Kensington, for example, wrapped in their massive money-nets, half-hidden behind walls or guarded by porter's lodges whose doors gleamed with polished brass. But they at least provided the pleasure of contrast. She was also rigid in her conception of what constituted the city. She loathed any hint of the suburban and anywhere not walkable from Charing Cross was to her impermissible, automatically transformed into somewhere else, not her *flâneur*'s metropolis but a dull district of parked cars and supermarkets and ashen-faced commuters at the close of day.

This is not the description of an idyll, but they lived a life that suited them both. They did not believe that they were smug – the usual indictment of those who have worked out a successful *modus vivendi* – for each of them knew well enough from experience what the opposite of this life was like and the shape it could easily resume at a moment's notice.

And they had their quarrels to keep them sharp and mettlesome.

Christopher considered that he enjoyed his work, which might be described as the plucking of order from chaos. The city was constantly renewing itself. Capital, one of his business partners once observed, grows lazy until it is woken from its sleep and reminded that there are things to be done, new opportunities to seize. Buildings were there to be bought and sold, refurbished or destroyed. Rebuilt from their own ashes. Old factories, dairies, dispensaries, their original purposes sometimes inscribed in ceramic tiles or garlanded in swathes of stone acanthus, were refashioned by clever designers and architects into new uses. Forty yellow tables with their accompanying tubular steel chairs were loud with diners on new Mediterranean cuisine in an old Zion chapel somewhere off the Tottenham Court Road. A scruffy Greek restaurant whose long lease had expired was now an aseptic gallery of costly artists' prints. Christopher waxed fat on all this ripping up and tearing out. He was quick and worked well to the blueprints provided. He had assembled a good team with whose help he would rip through the latest commercial premises, sizing, squaring, anticipating problems, juggling with solutions, taking pleasure in accommodating imperfections, protrusions, departures from exact angles. His clients were bracingly ruthless – unlike the slow, ruminative, rustic commissioners of unnecessary window-work whose fickle minds had changed from week to week. They were appreciative of his quick, provisional, extemporising skills. Every day on which interest was paid, and turnover deferred, worked on their angst, agitated their whole sensibility. They

walked into the devastation of floorspaces, lean and
hungry, wanting to know how much longer he would be,
what corners could be cut, what dead branches could be
lopped from the specification to speed fresh growth. At
their heels the next set of professionals waited, champing at
the bit, eager to pay their tribute of finishing skill to the
whole project, to bring nearer the moment when the tills
started to ring, the cards began to be swiped through the
jaws of the Visa machine like a sharpening blade.
Christopher felt like a pioneer hacking back the under-
growth at the edge of the last settlement. He was riding
high. He was intoxicated. He was part of the energy and
action in this city.

He asks himself: what happened, Carmen? How did we
contrive to cancel this bacchanale? He asks the questions
but he already knows the answers. The answer.

Christopher was hardly aware of Jimmy when he slid,
deftly, into their lives, smiling, unrolling the soft, luxurious
carpet of his charm, the famous charm that had caused so
many to give themselves to him, prodigally, eagerly, without
restraint and against their better judgement, when judgement was not the issue. Christopher and Carmen had
opening night tickets at Kerkyra in Museum Street.
Carmen swept in from work with her glossy black hair –
longer now – clamped at the back in a sapphire ring of elas-
ticated silk, turning every head in the crowded room. A
type with long hair tied in a pigtail was plucking a mandolin
in the corner. The lighting was subdued. Christopher's
olive-green counter was strewn with seductive nibbles and
ranged with complimentary glasses of house Mantinia.
Waitresses hung back, ready for their assault. A new wave
of Greek cuisine – taking the old staples and giving them
an expensive gloss – was sweeping the capital. Captain
Corelli's in Old Compton Street had shown the way but

dozens had followed. Christopher himself had three commissions in the queue – mostly quick refits of a kind he could turn around in three days, bribed by the first of them to get the lads lined up for a classic weekend job: in on Friday night at six and the corks popping at Monday night's opening.

Out of the cool clatter of cutlery and glassware, Jimmy approached their table, smiling suavely, large hands extended. You noticed the hands, of course, for they were Jimmy's trademark, his USP. That memorable CD cover of Berg, Schoenberg and Webern, with the elongated, delicate hands poised over the keyboard, had been a catchy icon after it won a *Gramophone* award and was advertised on the Underground – itself a rather remarkable achievement for three alumni of the Viennese School. Jimmy knew how to manage his success, how to play the admiring fish. He knew just how far to go and when to hold back. It was a performance as impressive in its way as his conduct at the piano. Like everyone else, Christopher and Carmen ate, eagerly, out of his hand. Unlike some celebrities who keep a dim recollection of those they have met – their real interest centring on themselves – Jimmy had remembered Carmen from the hotel on the Riviera. Christopher could see that Jimmy was homing in on her – although he was scooped up into the general embrace – and she warmly rose to take those magnificent hands. He smiled, offered them the gracious tribute of himself, wordlessly, for several seconds, then, after a quick acknowledgement of his encounter on the Riviera with Carmen, nodded with the faintly arch grace of a *maître d'*, and backed away to his table where he rejoined the glittering couple with whom he had come to dine. Christopher could not help noticing that he was unaccompanied.

Carmen responded testily to Christopher's inquiries. He could see that she detected the false note, his effort to appear detached, amused. She knew what he was thinking. What he was fearing. The ground was being cleared for a real humdinger but it was too early in the evening to launch the first strike. They attacked instead a small dish of varied dips – crushed walnut, taramasalata, something unidentified which, had he been able to stomach the preposterous prose of restaurant menus, Christopher could have had named. It was perhaps half an hour later – when he was quietly and intently at work on a challenging preparation of lamb – that Jimmy softly reappeared. He was off, it seemed, not staying for the full meal. His manner suggested more pressing business elsewhere. He had done what needed to be done. He dropped on to the tablecloth a flyer for a concert at the Purcell Room: John Cage's sonatas for prepared piano. They compliantly murmured that they would be there.

Over coffee, the first missile was launched.

"So, tell me more about the divine Jimmy."

"What is there to tell?"

"He seemed very pleased to see you."

Carmen looked at Christopher with that magnificent plaiting of pity and contempt that was her invariable starter.

"He's a professional charmer. He's pleased to see everyone."

"They seem to reciprocate. They don't seem able to resist him."

"Does that make you jealous?"

"What do you mean?"

"Forgive me, but I can't help sensing a little male rivalry here."

"What? The carpenter and the virtuoso? In which arena, tell me, would we be slugging that one out?"

"Don't be obtuse. You know exactly what I mean."

He knew exactly what she meant.

"No I don't. Why should I be jealous of that mountain of blue-eyed smarm?"

Carmen laughed in triumph. She had no further need of riposte.

"Are you going to his concert?"

"We could, I suppose, unless you have got one of your rush jobs on."

He didn't like her tone. It was uncertain, trying a little too hard for insouciance. It was patently obvious that she wanted to clock Jimmy again: the triumphant entrance through the narrow door at the rear of the stage (the Purcell, with its subtle intimacy, perfectly adjusted to Jimmy's special modes of self-display); the enveloping smile thrown out like a gossamer veil over the heads of the audience; the long, magnificent silent foreplay; the hand dragged back through the thick disordered thatch; then the first strike of the keys.

Of course he was fucking jealous.

One always wants to be above this, Christopher reflected. One wants to avoid pettiness. Nothing is more miserable than the accumulation of small resentments, suspicions, deliberate misprisions, with which lovers torment themselves when the going is unsteady. One wants to be magnanimous and at ease. Brimming over.

"So he met you in France?"

"Sure. Though I'm amazed he remembered me."

I shouldn't be scrutinising her, he thought, looking for tell-tale signs, shaky formulations, over-eager denials, making light of it.

"Would that be after I left?"

"Oh, please!"

"Sorry, but it's merely a casual inquiry. I hardly knew you at that time if you recall."

"You mean you hadn't yet established your rights of ownership."

"Don't be absurd."

"Look, Chris, I don't need this, right? You know perfectly well I can't stand this creepy possessiveness. I am a free agent and I expect you to be. I thought we weren't into all that sort of thing."

"I'm not saying we are."

"Well what the fuck are you saying, then?"

"Only that Jimmy seemed very familiar."

"But can't you see that he is like that with everyone, with all women. It's his way of doing things."

"You don't seem to object."

"Why should I object? It's up to him how he behaves. What do you want me to say? He's a sexist creep? OK, he's a sexist creep. Satisfied?"

"Fine."

"It's obviously not fine. What you want me to say is did I sleep with Jimmy at the Hotel Magnifique. And what I am saying is that I don't answer questions like that. In fact I object to their being put."

Christopher was reassured by her vehemence. She had not slept with Jimmy.

When the bill came, Carmen snatched it. In recognition of Christopher's services the wine had been on the house but the tally was still the equivalent of a week's income for a state pensioner. To them, this meant nothing, because they jointly earned more money than they could ever find the opportunity to spend. They were surrounded by countless others in the same predicament. They wanted to be able to spend more time with their possessions, longer at the yachting marina, more extended weekends in the Herefordshire cottage, more time gliding along the motorway network listening to audiobooks on the mellifluous in-car sound system. But the implacable ironmaster barked his orders at them and they continued to jump.

Christopher and Carmen walked back to Whitfield Street as they always did after a meal or a show, full of the vinous fumes of physical well-being. A resentful beggar, his blanket thrown over his shoulders like a mountain shepherd, cursed them as they passed. They had failed to notice him as they crossed Tottenham Court Road, their attention distracted by the need to avoid a drunk in an expensive suit who was pissing in the doorway of a computer shop. They slipped down a side street and turned in to the south end of Whitfield Street. A huddle of doubtful youths outside Crabtree Fields quickened their step and they were soon back at the flat. The quarrel about Jimmy had vivified them. They went straight to bed.

~

The audience at the Purcell Room was well-bred and middle-class, mostly middle-aged, but with a sprinkling of the younger generation – probably professional musicians, students, tyro composers. Christopher looked around the small chamber, noting how few people in this city of millions could be mustered for such an occasion. Jimmy – in black from head to toe but T-shirt and silk trousers taking the place of tuxedo and tails – handled the audience with aplomb. They loved it as much as he did and, of course, he played magnificently. Expecting to be bored or baffled, Christopher was enchanted by the spare rhythmic beauty of Cage's composition which he found ensnaring and irresistible. Whether Carmen at his side found music or musician irresistible was a matter of no consequence to him. He happily forgot where he was or any ground he might have for behaving in a resentful or peevish fashion.

At the end he applauded as vigorously as anyone else in the hall.

As they streamed away into the night, along the Embankment and over Charing Cross footbridge they said little. Jimmy was no longer an issue of contention between them. The air was sharp and appetising. They felt alive.

Inevitably, he reflected, I am cast as the pantomime villain. Let's blame Jimmy, the man who steals other people's partners. In fact, I steal no one. I have no interest in possession. They come to me of their own free will and I do not seek to hold on to them. But none of this is allowed. My function as scapegoat is too necessary for the prosaic truth to be allowed to complicate the imaginary record. How often have I seen myself not as a thief but as an arbitrator, stepping in between antagonistic parties, my services demanded peremptorily, sometimes without reward. It is not always pleasant, this sense of being ancillary to something that is happening elsewhere.

Nor am I, before we leave the metaphor of the stage, a Don Giovanni, a Casanova. The predatory male ceaselessly in pursuit of unattainable satisfaction, and destined, when time is called, to be swallowed by the jaws of hell. My amatory career began in the feminist 1970s and 1980s when the relations between the sexes were an arena of contest, challenge and mutual recrimination. In spite of my critics, I claim that I learnt from these arguments. I modified my practice but I could not stop loving women. Nor could I see it in me to apologise for what seems to me an essential activity, a necessary part of the business of being human.

Carmen claims that Jimmy first encountered her in an expensive hotel in the south of France. He has no recollection of this. As he sees it, a series of random and inconsequential sightings in London led to their having lunch and, later, to some hurried and not entirely satisfactory assignations – once in a small hotel in West London which he found rather amusing if faintly theatrical. He felt that, contrary to the way in which the charge-sheet is customarily drawn up, it was he who was being used. Carmen interested him. Her sexual allure was obvious, but something else drew Jimmy to her. He was fascinated by her strangely combative personality. He was given the usual motor tour of her past (the pinched provincial beginnings, the convent girl's ritual rebellions etc etc) and listened as patiently as he could. These recitals generally bored him in ways that were hardly expressible. He preferred to live for the present and nothing could be more alien to him than these obsessive English fossickings in the dusty lumber-room of class – always an uncle who is a bit of a card, a father whose flaws are re-arranged to his advantage with the passage of time, a put-upon mother whose quiet heroism is somehow consid-ered an inspiration. He wanted to lean across and vigorously shake the composers of these retrogressive monologues – indeed that is exactly what he sometimes did – urging them to cut free from the past and march forward with a light spring in their step towards the bright prospect of the new day. They look at him with suppressed anger. "You do not understand." Most true, he reflected. Most true.

Jimmy and Carmen quarrelled – which he took to be normal behaviour for her. He cannot now remember whether there was any substance to their polemics. He doubted it. The point – the need – was simply to contend. She was more adept than he at this business. He was perhaps too emollient, too given to the superficialities of social charm – for which she had no time at all. Frequently, he was taken aback by her rasping vehemence, her apparent determination to be as unwinning as possible, as if the faded fragments of old-fashioned courtesy, to which everyone else in various degrees clung in a coarsening world, were a kind of mocking offence to her, an additional aggravation. A kind of weakness. He gathered that her relations with Christopher were regulated by this kind of behaviour, certain stand-up rows in public places having become legendary in their circle.

Perhaps it was no more than the fascinated attraction of opposites that led Jimmy to tolerate – to wish to explore – this prickly young woman. There was also a certain energy about her which captivated him. She was ruthless – and ruthlessly cynical – in her practise of her profession. She talked about it with a vivid contempt that made him wonder how she could continue to practise it. He had encountered this before with other bright young women who found themselves unable to play the part which their colleagues played, to bring off the trick of convincing themselves that the daily inanities of the workplace were in fact as important to the world as the manoeuvres of high international diplomacy.

It is a handicap he considered that he faced as a performer (an 'arts worker' as he saw his like referred to in a recent newspaper) that he moved in a world of aesthetic pleasure, engaged each day in activities of patent worth. Aside from the occasional magazine interview or public relations call, he was not required to play games with himself, to pretend that what he was doing had a meaning which his inner self refused to endorse. He was happy and fulfilled in his work. His concerts gave him enormous pleasure and his commitment to new work, to breaking down the barriers of resistance to it, offered further satisfaction. He realised how lucky he was to experience this sensation. He knew how miserable many people were in their jobs. He saw it in their aggressive – if not hysterical – declarations of how much they enjoyed what they did. Carmen would speak of her employers and of her assignments with the most devastating contempt. Her intelligence became visible – vivid, outraged, traduced by the commissions it was compelled to accept. He asked himself – he was not yet ready to put the question directly to her – why she persisted. He could only assume that she had identified this world as one whose conquest she must achieve. She must have the scalp. Thus, the best and brightest of her generation went into these 'glamorous' media professions whose output was found so grimly disappointing, so unworthy of the attention of their intelligent peers.

One reason for the frequency with which Jimmy embarked on new liaisons – aside from his inextinguishable love of liberty – is that he came to feel that he knew his partner too well. He scented the danger of becoming bored. Anticipating objections, he conceded that the feeling may well have been mutual. Perhaps it is so in all cases. With Carmen it was different. Knowing her was like entering a receding prospect. The more time he spent with her, the less he seemed to know her. Her contradictions flowered like some odorous bloom in the *jardin des plantes*. This tantalised him and drew him on. He wanted to know more, he wanted to be satisfied that she made sense. With hindsight he felt that he had failed in that endeavour. She remained the enigma that she presented to him at their first meeting.

Sometimes he would play for her and watch, with minute attention, her reactions. There was a short Schoenberg piece – the Suite for Piano, op.25 – which he would play because she had expressed enthusiasm for it. It was not a long piece – perhaps no more than fifteen minutes – but she would sit for the duration on the edge of her seat, craning forward, tensed, suddenly tossing her head upwards when the music changed to a more abrupt tempo, subsiding, imperceptibly, when it became *etwas langsam*. After he stopped, she would be silent for several minutes, rocking gently, before springing up as if to shake off the surrender she had made to the power of the music. There is something magnificently cold, hard-edged, metallically brilliant about this piece which was plainly to her taste. Once, in a whitewashed warehouse-studio in Docklands where he was preparing for a recording session the following day, she sat on a slightly soiled cream-coloured sofa, spotlit by a shaft of sunlight which streamed through the high glass roof, and he reflected that never before had he enjoyed such an attentive listener. After the silence, he locked the door of the studio, which they had to themselves, and they made love in those beams of light, feeling the warmth of the sun on their naked skin, their bodies pressed against the hard, shiny wooden blocks of the floor.

She accused him – it was during a weekend which they had awarded themselves in Nice – of "patrician indifference", a charge which amused him at the time. In a sense, Jimmy reflected, she was right. His father had been a banker, immensely wealthy yet immensely distrustful of wealth. He had a puritan dislike of excess and lived simply in a way that only the very rich can bring off successfully. His one extravagance (and it was probably a concession to Jimmy's mother) was the flat on the seafront at Nice. He would have preferred to spend his retirement in Geneva or Paris but his wife aspired to the south of France. He loathed the town – its municipal corruption, the spectacle of all those leathery women of a certain age in white trouser suits, their gold bracelets jangling, as he put it "like the manacles of condemned prisoners", and the disgusting yapping pooches which they clasped to their blotched bosoms. He took refuge in his books and paintings, occupying one end of the five-roomed apartment in a magnificent austerity whose white walls became a sort of shifting inner screen on which his memories and recollections were projected. Sometimes Jimmy remembered this whiteness shimmering with a solitary blue canvas of Picasso, at another time it was a slender bronze scuplture on a marble base resting on a small side-table. In a room adjacent to this study, Jimmy's father slept beneath a tall window with a view of the sea. He spent his days back in the study, whose hushed and reverent silence the boy always hesitated to enter. Jimmy left for his international, drifting life of the concert performer not long after his parents settled in Nice, but when they died (the car spinning off the road somewhere north of Ventimiglia) he spent some time there, sorting their effects. He sold the Picasso and bought a flat in Regent's Park in a rather too solid mansion block. He would never pay rent again. He placed the Nice apartment with a smarmy lettings agency but not before he and Carmen spent a long weekend there. It was the site of their first quarrels.

She was vexed, he later realised, by what she called his "languid" demeanour. Perhaps too she regretted the fact that he was not a driven soul, anxious to make his mark, to establish himself, to hoist aloft the trophies of public approval. Born with a silver spoon crammed into his mouth (her locution), he was indifferent to the baubles, the awards, the tinsel decorations that start to drape, at an exponential rate of increase, the shoulders of the success-ful, often at the point when their triumphs are almost over. She seemed to believe that, since life had been difficult for her, it should be difficult for everyone else. More than this, she felt that difficulty, obstacle, the heroic jumping over these fences, were intrinsic to real achievement. It was Jimmy's denials, his insistence that art bestowed its gifts equally on the struggling aspirant and the easeful oaf, that angered her. He even went so far as to suggest that some of her examples of overcoming were specious – that far from triumphing over insuperable odds some of these sturdy folk had triumphed rather too easily. She exploded.

"How can you say that? How dare you say that?"

She waved her hands around the apartment, calling on its faux Empire trimmings and ornate picture frames (they were seated at his mother's end of the property) to witness the force of her logic. Both their eyes fell on a crusty gilt frame inside which a bright beach scene (a Sidley destined that week for the auction house – Jimmy did not trust the future lessees) glowed. A blue sail, a yellow expanse of sand, a shimmering parasol, the folds of a long white muslin dress, all conspired to rebuke and to repudiate his lack of understanding, his patrician indifference to the fate of the suffering classes.

"You sit there, basking in all this..."

There was a pause while she fumbled for some withering term that would be adequate to the enormity of this display of ill-deserved wealth, but nothing came.

"It's disgusting."

Cheaply, he leaned forward and refilled her slender champagne bumper, smiling complacently as the wine gurgled and frothed from the bottle.

"You miss the point, Carmen."

"Which is?"

"That we are all the product – I hesitate to use the term victim – of our backgrounds. We are never consulted about the circumstances of our birth."

She spat out her next contribution with a magnificent venom which he found thrilling.

"So you would have preferred to have been born in a two-up, two-down in Oldham."

"You hardly make it sound an enticing prospect."

"Oh for fuck's sake stop being so urbane. You know exactly what I mean. Of course you can't help being what you are, having had the advantages you have had. I am talking about some modicum of empathy. Some recognition that there are people in the world for whom all this..."

Another magnificent, sweeping gesture of contempt directed towards the interior décor, so vehement that the left hand came to the assistance of the right in keeping the champagne glass upright.

"...is not automatically assumed. May never even be seen or heard or smelt or touched or tasted."

"All five senses ticked off. All dues fully paid. All outrage registered."

"What the hell do you mean? Don't you grasp *anything* I have been saying?"

"Of course I do. But what do you expect from me? A formal recantation? A little pageant of self-loathing out of the Cultural Revolution? I am what I am. I agree that the world is unfair, that the rich are loathsome and vulgar (evidence of which, incidentally, I have had more opportunity than most to see at first hand). But I can't undo my experiences. I can't pretend that my life was different. In fact I'll go further and say that the music lessons in that lovely house in Zürich, the holidays in magnificent hotels across southern Europe, the gardens and drawing rooms, the music and paintings and constant immersion in things of beauty, the sheer variety and richness of that life, were glorious and I am glad to have had them. They stimulated me and filled my life with light and colour. I *enjoyed* them."

This was a little excessive, he knew.

Jimmy watched Carmen's reaction, trying to read the runes of her silence. In truth he felt she was being unfair. He had, after all, set up the Foundation for Young Musicians with the residue of his parent's estate (after deducting a generous amount for his own continuing welfare). As capitalist swine went he felt he could point to others more swinish. But he disliked what he called this moral pornography, this flaunting of one's keener ethical sense. He had decided to settle for the patrician indifference as a manner or style. He had no wish to be unctuous.

After this skirmish, Jimmy suggested going for a drive in the hired car. They sped off along the coast road in the direction of Monaco. As they took those twisting corners, the breeze streaming through the windows, he felt her mood soften. She shook out her hair with pleasure and excitement like a frisky pony and began to talk about having come this way as a young student on the train. She had changed to another train at the border and pressed on south. Her carriage was shared with two nuns and a pious looking couple who basked in the nuns' nimbus of sanctity. As the train approached Rapallo a wizened old codger had risen to his feet. He looked down at the glittering sea. Enraptured, he exclaimed:

"Che bel mare! Limpido!"

This, thought Jimmy, was the Carmen I loved so briefly, for whom I incurred the enmity of poor, wretched Christopher, whose life with her I broke up and destroyed. After both of us she disappeared. Out of the ruins of jealousy and anger she renewed herself and then was lost to us. A mere six weeks in my life but they left a more powerful impression than any other human being has left. It might have been longer had that day ended differently, had it not cast its long shadow (never admitted, never articulated) on our pleasure, but the chance happenings that destroy happiness proceed from the same beginnings as those which launch it in triumph. You see, he rebuked himself inwardly, how I remain the cracker-barrel philosopher?

The car sped on. They laughed. They touched. They passed a white coupé parked in a little viewing-space. A perfect couple, as if posing for a fashion plate, stood by their car looking out to sea. A pink chiffon scarf flew from her neck like a pennant. He was directing his video-camera at the rocky precipice below. Along here there were several such viewpoints. Jimmy and Carmen began to search for a suitable place to stop. She picked up his hand. He moved it to touch her thigh. An oncoming tour bus sounded its horn at them. Perhaps he had strayed too near to the central road marking or perhaps this was a gallant jest, a ribald tribute to the lovers' louche caress. He was careless. They were both careless, sensing no doubt, the heady imperative of *carpe diem*. He would shoot quick glances across at her, play with her fingers, return his eye to the wheel. As they came round a rocky corner, a viewpoint became visible. There was one car parked there but room for one more. He started to brake. The family was gathering around the boot of the car for drinks, laughing and excited like them. A little girl of perhaps five or six, pretty and blonde, her feet in white sandals, suddenly skipped out from the edge of the parking-bay as they continued their long, slow braking movement. Eyes on the rest of the family ahead, Jimmy had not seen her. She seemed to come precipitately from nowhere. He was still travelling quite fast in the wake of his impulsive decision to stop.

How often since had he been haunted by the sound of that soft knock, the sight of the little body thrown to one side like a discarded bag of picnic refuse. The scream, the swinging around in disbelief of the family at the car, the explosion of shock at what had happened, the force of it surging through a barrier of disbelief, the unmitigated horror as Jimmy and Carmen jolted forward in their seats from the final abrupt halt. The seconds of realisation, anguish, uncontrollable distress would give place to an aftermath of waiting in hospital corridors, being interviewed by cold and sceptical police officers, struggling to approach the parents in their renewed grief when it was announced by the doctors that everything was over.

Jimmy still hears the stifled sobbing of Carmen, who

could not get out of the car, frozen as she was by shock. She wanted to go. He had of course to stay (after some initial uncertainty he was informed that no charges would be brought) but, after insisting that she wait until at least the next morning, he let her go. He thought that this would be for ever, that she would go back to Christopher. This is what she did, but not immediately, and not, as it turned out, irrevocably, for he would see her again in London. These events became a subject about which they could not talk, though he would gladly have done so.

The newspaper reports, inevitably, referred to what happened as "a tragedy". At the time, Jimmy considered that the dull cliché for once was right. It is in the nature of classical tragedy to make human life seem predestined. Things happen on those bare, anguished stages because they must happen, because the Gods insist on a pattern of retribution and justice, a particular conclusion. This terrible, needless death seemed connected – in ways he could not articulate exactly – with the fleeting hedonism of those few days in Nice. It was as if they needed to be taught that their lives were tangled up with the lives of others, that if they overreached themselves in the selfish glut of pleasure there would be a price to pay. He should have liked to try this interpretation out on Carmen but for now she was gone. And as the days and weeks passed he began to retreat from this grand theory. He felt only intermittent pain and remorse, logic giving place to the stab of isolated images – the tearful parents at the hospital, the little coffin lowered by tapes into the ground, Carmen, shaking uncontrollably at his side in the immediate aftermath, resisting the comfort of the hand he extended to her.

Christopher's latest amour is just ending after seven tempestuous days (seven times longer than his average dalliances – for that is now what they have come to seem). Catriona is in public relations. She is mistress of the argot of her profession. When they go to bed she brings her mobile to the bedside, laying it down with care, as a mother might anxiously position her child's crib within reach should its crying in the night demand her attention. In place of the soft warble of his bedside telephone, Catriona's device erupts with a martial trumpeting like that of a crowd of cinema Cossacks hurtling in savage vengeance across some arid steppe, sabres raised to catch the flash of the sun, leering triumph in every horseman's eye. Just now, he listened to her conversation with a 'work colleague'.

"Hayley, love, we've got a toughie here but I know you are up for it. These people are in the stone age. We are going to have to do some work around the issue of appropriate language for starters. I'll email you my thoughts in the morning."

Still turning over those 'thoughts' in her mind, she undressed, mechanically, as if stepping into a shower, not into the arms of her soon-to-be-redundant lover. Christopher wondered, as they tussled, how far behind she had left that crusade against inappropriate language. Certainly, next morning, as they conducted their weak hostilities, which ended in mutual letting-go, he felt that her lack of stomach for a fight had more to do with that email of worked-on thoughts, her electronic battle-plan, than with any incapacity for the polemical side of love. From the diamond glint in her eye he felt that she was already else-where. As the door closed he fell back in lassitude on a kitchen chair. Above the clatter of heels on the stair he could hear the cry of the first cavalry charge of the day.

Many of the young women with whom Christopher tried to recreate the passion he had known with Carmen – a doomed and desperate mission – shared this braced eagerness for work. It was a word which they used, not with the cynicism of old lead-swingers, duty-dodgers, free-wheelers, escapees, nor with the oppositional force of the historical radicals hoping to liberate the working man and woman from hated chains, but with a kind of whooping triumph. They loved their work and their employers loved them for that amatory gift. It gave them sense and purpose and a moral compass in a world of lost directions and aban-doned distinctions. I am what I do. As an alternative to the terror of ennui, the pain of living inside the prison house of self, it was the sweetest option, requiring only complete surrender of the will to the imperative of the workplace. An effortless bargain. In exchange, they would receive status, hard cash, a tight, sure frame into which they could pack their youthful energies. This, it seemed to him as he drew patterns in spilt coffee on the melamine top of the kitchen table, was why they seemed so manically alert. They had something bright and glittering in their sights and they were going for it with vigour and excited pleasure. It was a world of clear present light – not a world of half-shadow and nuance, touched by the breath of history, fitful glimpses of the submerged alp of possibilities, the far-off mutter of other voices.

It was not our world, Carmen, he told himself. She also could be known by her martial zest, her wild, quarrelsome vigour. But this was to omit her ability to give, her startling generosity of spirit. No longer bathed in its wash of light, he considered that he had grown more meagre. He was wasting away. He needed the *aqua vitae* of her presence. Instead, he drank the brackish water of her absence.

When Carmen came back from Nice – she would not tell Christopher where she had been, or what had happened there, though he was sure that something quite distressing had taken place – they tried to mend the torn fabric of themselves by going away together. It worked. Abandoning their lives to the care of answering machines and the thickening snowfall of accumulating electronic messages, they spent fourteen days rediscovering themselves. The process was easy. It was like coming to a country house locked up for the winter. One has only to put the key in the lock, kick away the circulars and meagre mail from behind the door, pull off the dustsheets, light a fire in the cold, dusty hearth, sweep mouse-droppings from the kitchen drawers, quickly start a simple meal on the hob, open a bottle of wine reached down from the shelf where it has lain since the last visit. Once again Christopher and Carmen surprised each other with the reminder that, after all their frantic city agendas, nothing had changed in the remote landscape of their inner lives, its quiet motions still unrolling, the same trees in leaf, bright with new growth, the same sound of the brook running down the side of the adjoining meadow. That odd miracle of instant forgetting was re-enacted.

They chose, after the briefest of debates, an island in the Sporades. The ferry docked at a tiny mole on which only a dozen people were waiting: an old couple lugging boxes fiercely tied up in string, a quickly trotting Orthodox priest with a long black beard who was nearly too late for the impatient boat, a motorcylist, a dusty lorry, several idlers or fishermen. They were the only passengers to disembark.

With a peremptory hoot the ferry backed away and was soon steaming on to its remaining destinations. As they walked towards the waterfront its beauty silenced them. The houses were painted in white or in light pastel shades. There were few people about. The season for visitors having barely begun, they feared that they might have difficulty finding rooms, but an inquiry at the only open bar resulted in gestures, shouting, then the appearance, apparently from nowhere, of a middle-aged woman in black. She had an amused, ironic air. She led them up an open stairway to a room with a direct view of the harbour and the sea. It had clearly not been used since last season but she made the motion of a broom and grinned. They squeaked open the windows opening on to the balcony, scraped up two white plastic chairs, wiped off some bird lime, and sat down to breathe the lovely morning air, delighted at the warmth of the sun on their pale northern skins. At that moment, Carmen, Christopher reflects, I did not wish to be anywhere else, holding cupped in my hands the bright fluttering butterfly of present pleasure. I think you shared my desire. I think you would recall that moment were I to offer it to you now. But I cannot do so. I do not even know where to find you.

Unthinkable, then, such an outcome.

Each morning they would perform their ritual visit to the *artopoieio*, coming back with fresh bread to make their own coffee in the *briki* that hung in the small communal kitchen at the end of the corridor, all the rooms as yet uninhabited. Their arrival had acted as a catalyst. They heard the scrape of beds, the clatter of plastic dustpan on terrazzo floor, and the hosing down of chairs. The season was slowly declaring itself open. Their days were spent in delicious languor. After breakfast they would saunter up and down the waterfront, engaged on trivial and specious errands, then move slowly towards the beach or take a pack of bread, olives and a thin wedge of hard cheese up into the wooded hinterland where roseate craggy rocks hung over the twisting track and where they would climb for half a day before being driven down by the heat to a refreshing immersion in the transparent water of the pebbly beach. In the afternoons they would doze fitfully, or sit on the now shaded balcony reading their bulky paperbacks. What lessons, Christopher wonders, did I learn that fortnight from the plump pages of *I Promessi Sposi*? In the evenings, showered and changed, they would descend to the bar for a milky ouzo, then walk to the opposite end of the front to the single restaurant where they chose stuffed tomatoes or fresh fish, washed down with no doubt too many jugs of wine from the great dark barrel at the back of the cool interior of the taverna.

And afterwards what lovers do, holding each other lightly, too sedated by this Sybaritic regime to detour into their customary verbal skirmishing. Looking back, from the ruin of his present existence, Christopher considered that the memory of this was almost sufficient to redeem what came after. He told himself that he had received his due, more than his due, and that it was mere greed, mere peevishness, to insist on coming back for more. He must learn that lesson. He must learn to let her go. Carmen's disappearance may have been the better part of wisdom. Perhaps, after all, it was not from cruelty but from having his interests at heart that she discharged him. Made mellow by these recollections he will agree to anything. He saves the hangover for his bitter awakening in the small hours.

Jimmy, however, he cannot forgive. That was palpable cruelty. Carmen allowed herself to grow apart from him, to extend towards the other's sun for – what? A brief affair that lasted only weeks and which destroyed everything they had built. Yes, yes, they spoke of freedom. They repudiated possessiveness. They held on to their rights. But surely that was mere rhetoric? They did not believe – Christopher did not believe – that it would be put to the test. That either of them would act on it. Carmen gave herself to him, she made him the recipient of her marvellous gift and he tossed it back to her, hardly used. This he did not understand.

It has already been made clear that discord was the aphrodisiac cordial they quaffed. But on one occasion at least they became a splendid team of two. Before launching his career as a fashionable metropolitan shopfitter, Christopher had dabbled in photography. There had also been spells of teaching, pottery, landscape gardening – had he not also put on, for a season, the roomy trousers and peaked cap of a municipal park-keeper? Postgraduate qualifications in the literature of the Spanish-speaking peoples had quite disabled him from any proper and sustained employment. The photography had lasted for as long as six months. He had taken pictures of other people's gardens for a range of horticultural and 'leisure interest' magazines – at the bottom end of that particular market. Now, Carmen was keen to use his services, for the good reason that he was very cheap. Her fitful ambition was to break out of the trivia of young women's journalism (though Christopher always admired her skill in picking up the latest trends, mastering instantly the appropriate language) and launch herself as a serious broadsheet writer, profiling the better class of celebrity.

The problem she and her editors faced was that of a diminishing number of potential subjects. All the big game had been captured. In addition, the pool of celebrity was being re-stocked with inferior fish. The link between fame and talent having been more or less severed, a subject could be invented overnight, thus staving off shortages. But there was sometimes a problem, even with the more optimistic features editors, in convincing readers that they had heard of the celebrity being wheeled out into position. In short, there was no shortage of minnows but where were the leaping salmon, the savage-toothed pike? One solution to the problem was the sub-genre of rediscovered celebrity. Ancient relics of Bloomsbury who had an anecdote or two to tell about Dorothy Brett or Maynard Keynes or Virginia Woolf (involving with luck a sexual misdemeanour or a scabrous *mot*) were particularly well-received. It gave the reader a pleasant frisson to think of how brittle was the platform on which fame rested. Set against today's ubiquitous trollop was the wizened oldster who had slept with HG Wells and now lived obscurely in Somerset in a cottage thick with books and dusty oils by forgotten Edwardians who were once the outriders of the avant-garde. The appeal was that of ancient manners, patrician hauteur, and old venom recapitulated in perfect sentences. A feminist critic who had been a university contemporary of Carmen's tipped her off about Lavinia Watersmith, whose solitary novel, *Absent From Felicity* (1931) was about to be re-issued by a new post-feminist imprint.

"Yes, but where *is* Great Malvern?" Christopher asked Carmen in a tone which nonetheless implied that his consent was taken for granted. He told her that he had a new job starting in three days' time so they had better move quickly.

Carmen, a city girl to the core of her being, was unable to answer his question without recourse to a large, flapping road atlas. Since Miss Watersmith's diary was not, these days, crammed as tight as a city banker's with important assignations, she was able to accommodate them the following day. They were at Paddington station next morning at 8.30 a.m. Christopher was warned to hold his tongue, avoid calling her "Mizz", and be on the look-out for good framing shots. There was at least one Carrington painting in the house and, it was rumoured, a rare portrait of Lytton Strachey by a talent so obscure that neither of them could hold the name in their minds longer than the time taken to be told it over the phone by Carmen's academic buddy.

Two hours after leaving Paddington, the train pulled in to a delightful station, rather like those one had as a child in a railway set. Yellow stone, cast iron pillars wrapped around by fruiting vines in coloured tin, a few bewildered Japanese tourists, and a mad Worcestershire aboriginal in a white open-necked shirt mouthing imprecations at anyone who would listen, all greeted them as they disembarked. As if to suggest that this was quite far enough for any civilised person to venture, the train immediately prepared to reverse for the return journey to London. There were no taxis in the designated rank so they set off on foot through leafy streets flanked by large, solid houses. A pall of suffocating gentility hung over the town, whose inhabitants seemed universally ancient and well-to-do.

"We are in the heart of middle class, middle England, my sweet," Christopher informed Carmen in a tone of thin sarcasm.

"Makes you want to head straight back to the Smoke."

"What are we looking for?"

"Albion Villa, Hyacinth Drive."

"Is that for real?"

"It's what it says here."

Soon they stopped a ruddy local in mirror-bright brown brogues and a pale green tweed jacket in whose V was lodged an efflorescent yellow Paisley cravat. Ebulliently, he turned them round and gestured towards the distance and Hyacinth Drive, third on the left. In his excitement he dropped a string bag of library books, causing his small Scots terrier in its tartan cummerbund to break into a fit of shrill yapping. They thanked him and darted away.

"Quiet, Monty! Quiet, there's a good chap!"

Carmen spoke for them both when she observed that this had better be worth it. Hyacinth Drive turned out to be a steep ascent towards the base of the Malvern Hills. The substantial late Victorian villas – with their high protective shrubberies, solid gates built to withstand the intruder, and their air of quiet, self-assured dulness – retreated from the sloping road, being reachable by asphalted drives of a gradient even steeper than that of the Drive itself. Albion Villa eventually hove into view. It was much like the others, though its paintwork was in a poorer state of repair, and the garden was slipping easily into a state of urban wilderness. Brightly coloured weeds poked out of the fissures in the asphalt, and the front gate lacked several of its supporting struts. They marched up to the front door which turned out to be open. A small shrill voice called from within:

"Is that you, Miss O'Hare? Do please come in. The door is open."

Tentatively, with that extravagant slowness of movement – tender smirks, condescending sweetness of manner – with which we behave when approaching the elderly and infirm, Carmen and Christopher crossed into the hallway. A gloriously blue canvas crossed by a solitary white gull winging above a trough of yellow sand filled the whole of the left-hand wall, quite diverting their eyes from the threadbare carpet.

Miss Watersmith, her white hair disordered as if she had been caught in a stiff gale at sea, smiled welcomingly at them, her veined and knobbled hands gripping tightly a light aluminium Zimmer frame. She looked like a benign little bishop about to deliver a sermon from the pulpit. She wore a loud orange dress of delicate silk which must have been quite a hit in 1947. She cocked her head in the direction of the front room which opened off to the right.

"I'll be with you in a moment. Do make yourselves comfortable. Mrs Meredith has been so kind and laid out our coffee things. If you could be so kind as to pour us all out some coffee, Mr..."

"Wilson."

"That would be most kind. I am afraid that I take such a long time to complete anything these days."

And then she laughed (having moved about three feet into the room):

"But time, contrary to the conceits of the poets who would see me hastening to the grave, is what I seem, these days, to have in abundance. I can happily spend half an hour getting up to consult a dictionary for one word. When I was young I seemed to have no time at all. We lived, you know, in such an unconscionable whirl. We were so *fast*. But now I am inundated with time. The days are so long. And Charon and his dark boat are nowhere to be seen."

They laughed a little too enthusiastically.

"I expect you have come to hear me prattle about my days with Virginia. That's what they all seem to want to hear now. It's an awful thing to say but I didn't really like her at all. She was so bluestockingy, and such a wicked gossip. That was the thing I didn't like about that set. So malicious in their gossip. It really wasn't necessary. I think that they didn't really care for ordinary human kindness. There was something cold and brittle about them all. But oh, so immensely clever and so witty and so entertaining when they wished to be. I expect we would all be the poorer without them."

Miss Watersmith had reached her high chair, transferring herself thither with a neat, pleasant little movement from the support of the Zimmer which remained parked in front of her. Christopher brought her a cup of coffee and another to Carmen. The Woolf anecdotes had been milked dry by previous expeditions up the dandelion-pocked drive. Carmen had already explained that there was nothing more to be had there. She intended to focus on the novel but her editor expected at least a few scraps of gossip that weren't already stowed in the cuttings file.

"Yes it's quite extraordinary," Lavinia continued. "To think that my little book should be given another outing and so late in the day. It was considered quite a controversial novel at the time of course. Compared to what one reads today or sees on the television it no doubt strikes you as very tame indeed. But even my buried hints at love between women were too strong for some stomachs. The moral reprovers are so good at picking up the merest hint of sexual unorthodoxy. I think their minds must dwell on it a great deal. When I look at it now I think perhaps that I made it too sentimental. The heroine is rather a drip, don't you think?"

As Carmen swung into action at this prompt Christopher began to withdraw his camera from its bag with the wily circumspection of a bagsnatcher. Lavinia looked across at him and waved her assent with a little playful gesture of the hand. He started to move around the room, waiting for the decisive moment. He was half listening to her talk.

"Of course we saw Mosley rather differently in those days. He was quite dashingly handsome and so many people felt in the 1920s and the 1930s that things were in such a frightful muddle that some stronger medicine was needed. The traditional prescriptions hadn't really worked. I suppose he offered a solution of sorts. With the benefit of hindsight we can see it was all wrong of course. But hindsight is something you never have at the time. I sometimes wonder if we don't need something a little more forceful now with all these dreadful strikes and so forth."

Carmen skilfully drew her Fabian heroine away from these jagged black rocks towards a calmer expanse of untroubled water. It was the Sapphic seam that she had been instructed to mine. "Politics are a complete turn-off for readers at the moment," her editor had warned her.

Christopher continued his prowling around the room like a child playing a game of hide and seek. He was reasonably confident that he had collected a sufficient number of revealing and/or quirky shots around which Carmen's text would wrap itself like a well-managed vine.

Eventually, Carmen concluded that she would get no more juice from this wrinkled lemon and stood up with, it seemed to Christopher, an unnecessary brusqueness. They offered to gather up the coffee things but Lavinia waved away their gesture.

"Mrs Meredith will deal with all that later. I don't know what I would do without her. She's Welsh, but very nice."

They retreated down the camber of her drive with their idiot smiles flashing like warning lamps. Back in the herbaceous street they conducted a quick post-mortem.

"You didn't get to the story about Virginia Woolf's knickers and the Henley Regatta?" he queried.

"If that anecdote gets another outing the public will scream."

They left Great Malvern in good spirits. The outcome, however, would be brutally disappointing. The piece was set up on screen yet spiked peremptorily by a new features editor who swept into the office on her first day determined to establish her authority by a casual show of violence. Carmen's profile was the first blood-sacrifice of the day. By then it was too late to offer it around to those few broadsheets who cared sufficiently about mid-twentieth century literature, all of whom either had decided Watersmith was an obscure relic or had commissioned their tie-in pieces already. Their little joint essay eventually found a home in a badly-produced literary quarterly emanating from North Shields where it appeared fourteen months later.

Carmen came back from Nice in a state of shock. That terrible business finished for the time being her affair with Jimmy (though a breeze would stir the embers into flame once or twice more). It was an accident. She found it hard to see that it could have been avoided, even if they had been more vigilant, less absorbed in each other. Even the parents of the dead child seemed to accept that this was so, blaming themselves, in spite of the protestations of Jimmy and Carmen, for not exercising more care over their precious child. She would wake, shaking, seeing the whole scene replayed with preternatural vividness, reliving its terror, night after night. Until, of course, it began to fade, slipping back into that repertory of casual horrors that the system of nightmares keeps for future use.

Christopher, towards whom she felt she had behaved so monstrously, was marvellous. Knowing nothing of what had happened and therefore freed from the need to express the usual fatuous reassurances, the sentimental clichés, he merely waited for her, listening, avoiding comment, allowing her to say what she needed to say, however halting and self-contradictory and exhausted her utterance. Carmen had gone straight back to him. He suspected that her deliberate vagueness about her reasons for going to Nice – a refusal that was not unusual between them, so fiercely did they cling to their freedom – covered something that would turn out to be painful for him. Perhaps for that reason he drew back from interrogating her, from seeking to know more. She decided not to come clean, saying only that she had witnessed a dreadful accident whilst staying with an old friend. She was sure that he was unconvinced by the detail but it suited him to go along with the general tenor of her explanation.

But something irrevocable had happened. Notwithstanding the freedom of their relationship, its absence of shackles and demands, an important barrier had been breached. Carmen had been seriously dishonest with Christopher. Deceit had now entered their mutual existence like a virus. Their life together would never be the same again. Perhaps that point can be identifed as the start of the process which led to its dissolution. If so, she considered that she had only herself to blame. But on those occasions when they had talked in the past – in the most general terms – about 'relationships' they had agreed that chance plays the greatest part and that the course of an involvement can often seem pre-destined, our own ability to steer it, to rescue it from disaster, turning out to be quite limited. In short, no one is to blame. No doubt a very convenient philosophy for some partners.

Carmen agreed to Christopher's suggestion that they take a fortnight in Greece. It was a way of avoiding morbidity – or the possibility of an approach from Jimmy for whom she was not ready – and it proved a success. She was drawn back to Christopher. They were closer during that fortnight than they had ever been. It is true that she was troubled by her deceit. She could not say to him just why he meant so much to her at that time. Her renewed affection for him was triggered by a remorse that could not be confessed but which, in some sense, she felt sure he understood. They gave themselves to the immediate moment, something that it was rarely possible to do in their London lives – they were so bound up with calculating self-interest and ambition. As Carmen lay on that raked, pebbled beach she turned over in her mind again and again the direction her life had taken and seemed likely to take in the future. It is not unusual, she felt sure, for people to consider that their lives have taken a wrong turning, even when they are decked in the livery of apparent success. She tried to impose a shape on what had already happened: the precocious student, the heroine of the neatly measured-out wild period, the reformed, promising post-graduate, then the reaction against an academic career, the pursuit of metropolitan success. To say that she was not satisfied misses the point. No one in her world, she considered, believed that they were satisfied. Indeed, the restless, manic energy, of those media trades was driven by unease, by a desire to break out from something unspecified into something else even more impalpable. Yet at the same time it was the continuous process that possessed Carmen and her colleagues. She would nonetheless gladly have changed places, taken up something more radically fulfilling. The problem was that she did not have the first idea what that desirable avocation might be.

After they returned Carmen resolved to take some small measures of amelioration. She would devote herself at least to the odd assignment that bespoke quality. That was what prompted her to take Christopher with her as photographer on the doomed assignment, whose chaotic outcome was one that she might have been able to predict. She went quickly back to her bright trash. To her dismay, she discovered she was getting better at it. The commissions came in such profusion that she was working harder than ever. She even won an award sponsored by a hairspray giant.

One evening Carmen was rung by an old friend. The call came as she sat with Christopher at an aluminium table set up outside an Italian coffee shop in Wardour Street. He joked that it was another of her lovers. She said sweetly that she did not usually choose her own sex. She and Alice met two days later at a restaurant in Southampton Row.

Alice had always been striking, but now she seemed to Carmen to have reached that level of casual perfection that one associated with legendary French film actresses who have discovered the means of outwitting time. She was dressed in the very simplest outfit of black which you knew instinctively (without being remotely able to guess at the house of couture which had sold it to her) to be very expensive. Her movements, her way of holding herself, gave away her profession. Carmen had always wondered how Alice survived in it. The model agencies seemed now to prefer anorexic waifs, street kids, the calculatedly dishevelled. Alice, a reprehensible twenty years older than these new fashion magazine icons, belonged to an older school of studied elegance. Even that word now rang a little false. But she was still in demand. There remained certain products which traded on a more traditional image of female beauty. She was just young enough, and just elegant enough, to appeal to the classier end of the market. She was also utterly without illusion. She knew that her days were numbered, that cool aplomb was one thing and that wrinkles, the resistless decay of the flesh, were another.

Carmen had assumed that, being in London briefly from her Paris base, Alice had been at a loose end and wanted simply to catch up with an old friend. But as they talked it became clear that something else was worrying her. The main course had barely arrived when she began to broach her real agenda.

"Did you know I was thinking of packing it all in?"

"But why? I thought you were at your peak. I must have seen you seven times going down the escalator at Green Park the other day."

"Oh God, that jewellery they made me wear was ghastly."

"Rather Versace, I thought."

"Don't mention that name in my presence."

"Is this a case of quitting while you're ahead?"

"Not exactly, but of course one has to be careful not to overstay one's welcome on the billboards."

"Then it's something else. I can't help noticing you've been silent on our usual topic."

"Oh, the love-life is still the same."

"I bet it is."

"Don't believe anything you read in the media about G____."

"So what's the new departure? Don't tell me you're writing a novel."

"Oh, Car, credit me with some IQ."

"Then what is it: revulsion at the shallowness of the fashion industry? But you were revolted by it before you even took your first trip along the catwalk."

"No, it's something else."

As they spoke, Carmen could see a change coming over Alice. Slowly, her trademark composure, the achieved poise that fashion editors could not stop falling for after all these years, crumpled, collapsed inward like a plastic beaker tossed on to a bonfire. For the first time Carmen saw a new side of her. She saw a kind of exhaustion, a sudden glimpse of vulnerability, uncertainty, confusion. Not perhaps so very different from expressions she had seen at moments of stress on the faces of other friends, but so wholly at odds with what she expected from Alice that it shocked her. Carmen waited for Alice to explain in her own time.

"I don't know whether any of this will make sense. I know that I will be accused of 'over-reacting'. The highly strung pedigree racehorse panicking in the viewing enclo-sure. That's usually how they deal with my outbreaks of feeling which, as everyone knows, I am not supposed to have. The glittering 'icon' is not meant to show any passion, to lose her cool. But what everyone forgets is that it is all a performance. It is put on. And sometimes one wants to put it off, to allow the real me to escape."

"That's usually a mistake, believe me. But we're all playing roles. Look at the stuff I churn out."

Alice looked at Carmen and laughed. It was an interval in the gloom. She had obviously read some of her friend's pieces, probably in magazines where the text threaded itself around the bodies of Alice's younger friends. Carmen reflected that she didn't expect Alice to show quite such ready endorsement of her self-deprecation.

"No, it's something more than the usual ritual self-loathing."

"Which comes with the turf."

"Exactly."

Carmen looked at Alice's hands. They were so perfectly shaped – giving the manicurist so little to do in the way of enhancement of their effect. She stretched them out in front of her as if she were calculating the value of an asset, an object. Her beauty, Carmen felt (not for the first time) was unsettling. Could one be almost too perfect?

"It happened about three weeks ago. I was coming up an escalator at Bond Street – just like you said a moment ago. It was that same poster."

"The one in the white knickers and the gold jewellery. The Egyptian slave look."

"Someone had..."

She faltered. Carmen wasn't sure whether to take her hand, to offer her some physical reassurance, but neither of them had ever been the touchy-feely type. Instead, she waited for Alice to pick herself up, to put herself back on course.

"Someone had scribbled some graffiti... across the... crotch."

She broke down. She whispered across the table the vile

little obscenity that some twisted mind had framed. Short, vicious, impregnated with hate for her sexuality, her womanhood. She took a deep slug of white wine and struggled to continue.

"It's not the first time, of course, it's often no more than an adolescent joke. One has to be used to it. It's a professional hazard and often a relatively minor one. After all, if you flaunt your body across the hoardings and the bookstalls, you can hardly justify maidenly outrage. The house rule is to take it all on the chin, to minimise it, to avoid being uncool. But there was something different about this. There was a kind of *virulence* about it that chilled me. Where do words – thoughts – like that come from? Are they just random, a lone nutter? Or is this widespread? If so, it frightens me."

"I'm sure there have always been people like this around."

"But I sense that it's ... deeper, somehow. I got a kind of chill off that, as if it were the tip of something, or a curtain pulled back on something very nasty indeed."

Carmen looked hard at Alice. She wasn't sure she was handling this very well. The obvious feminine solidarity was there. All women have known harassment and worse. Alice knew Carmen was on her side. And, naturally, these were topics she had sounded off enough about in her pieces over the years. But there was something else at work here. She was seeing the gradual removal of a brilliant, gilt-flecked veil and beneath it was a woman fearful and exposed. The Alice sitting across the table from her was not the Alice that the world knew. It was not the Alice that Carmen knew.

"The fact is, Car, I'm frightened. Frightened at what I've done."

"At what *you* have done!"

"Haven't I colluded in this, turned myself into an image of upmarket sexuality, offering an eyeful to every passenger on the Underground?"

"Oh, Alice, please! This is all wrong. You are a beautiful woman. You have added beauty to the world – think of those Bruce Neubauer pics. They're in the Museum of Modern Art for Christ's sake! Women shouldn't be required to cover themselves up, to deny their sexuality, their pleasure in how they are, just because a minority of men..."

Alice looked up and smiled through her tears.

"You once would have said a majority of men."

Their laughter dispatched much of the tension that had been building up. This time Carmen did find herself stretching her hand across the table, giving those beautiful hands a gentle squeeze.

"The fact is that I am through with this business. I suppose you never make a decision for one reason alone. It's been building up for some time. The disgust at the business is always there. Liked piped music in a department store. But I can see that I have only a limited amount of time. I am thinking of selling that tiny Manhattan apartment – do you remember, you stayed there – and making Paris my main base. And, yes, I have been talking to publishers, but about a sort of reminiscence."

"Well, you have met just about everybody."

"I think I can survive. There are all sorts of things I want to do and I'd rather choose to do them now than wait for them to be forced on me as a kind of survival strategy. I'd like to spend the next phase of my life doing some proper living. Perhaps that nasty little creature with the indelible pen has done me a favour after all."

Alice was slowly recovering, gathering up the scattered fragments of herself, re-establishing the customary poise. It was a subtly mingled process, physical and emotional, utterly riveting to watch. She kept drawing herself up, straightening her back, stretching out her arms, breathing deeply, running one of those slender beautiful fingers across her brow. When she had finished, when the process was complete, she turned her attention to Carmen.

"And what have you been up to? How's life with Christopher?"

"Oh, we've had our usual ups and downs. It's fine just now."

"Has there been anyone else?"

She interpreted Carmen's silence.

"So you've been a naughty girl again?"

"We've always been very open. Actually, that's not the right word. In some ways we're not open at all. We have always made a point of allowing ourselves as much..."

"Don't say it. 'Space'"

"You think I'm living out one of my 'lifestyle pieces'?"

"Possibly. But I shouldn't have interrupted."

"No, go on."

"You mean that you don't feel the need to tell each other everything. I've always been the same. It goes against the textbooks which say you have to share every damn thing. But I want the freedom to be myself in a relationship. To have secrets when I want them. Why should I have to tell everything."

"Your publishers will be expecting you to."

"That's different. That's for dosh, darling."

"You haven't changed."

"No, I suppose not. I've just decided to give a little more indulgence to the real me – if I know, after all these years, who that is. I've had a good run for my money. If I start to whinge tell me to be quiet."

They had now reached the end of their meal. The

waiters, drawn like moths to a lamp by Alice's beauty, had pestered them throughout with unnecessary inquiries – and that damned pepperpot the size of an elephant's phallus. They asked for the bill and exchanged up-to-date addresses. Alice ordered Carmen to come and see her in Paris. She was flying out first thing in the morning. There would be no time to see Christopher.

"Another time, darling," the fully-restored Alice purred as she flagged down a cab in New Oxford Street. She stepped into the back of the vehicle and waved regally, before popping her head through the window.

"Oh, by the way, I had a call from that gorgeous hulk, Jimmy, earlier in the week. He's got an engagement in Paris the week after next and he's going to look me up."

"Lucky you," Carmen called in a tone whose uncertain emphases were drowned out by the accelerating roar of the cab.

Christopher is sitting with his legs stretched out on the sanded but not yet polished wooden floorboards of his latest project: a cool, open-fronted bar on the edge of Covent Garden in Great Queen Street overlooking the portentous grey mass of a Masonic lodge – or do they call it, he wondered, a temple? Today he has been let down by his builders. Their failure to arrive has thwarted the next phase of his work. He is waiting for them to break open the frontage to create a set of folding glass panels. Without them, he is becalmed, tasting a very unusual hour or two of leisure. This is so rare as to be unsettling.

The sun is streaming through the old shop window that will be removed, perhaps later today, when the moonlighting contractors eventually arrive. It was a shop specialising in writing materials – gold-nibbed pens, unusual inks, heavy cream-coloured paper, portable leather writing cases. The gold lettering still catches the sunlight, traces the shadow of script on the floor in front of him. By the end of today that sheet of glass will lie shattered in the bottom of an iron builder's-skip.

Robertson's, in its day, was a legendary shop where one went when every other outlet had failed to satisfy one's quest. The staff were ancient – as is the rule in such old-fashioned places – and were characterised by a sort of lordly rudeness, as if their job were made disasteful to them by the oafishness of customers who were, increasingly, insufficiently educated in the complex rites of penmanship. They wore black waistcoats with shiny green silk backs, gold half-mooned spectacles, and moved about the shop with immense slowness, their great glistening domed pates catching the subdued light from brass lamps set at intervals between the fluted pilasters. Often, when they had found – after an initial display of scepticism – that they did indeed have the calibre of pencil-lead or the tint of ink sought, they would wrap it up with a wrinkle of distaste, as if they doubted that the purchaser realised the nature of what he or she was buying. They saw themselves as learned clerks in a culture of barbarism, their knowledge and their discriminating subtlety despised by a world which had no present use for such qualities.

When young Mr Angus Roberston, nephew of the founder, and a freshly awarded Harvard MBA, inspected the books, he announced the same day that the business would close at the end of the financial year. He was going into hand-held computers and all this antique rubbish was to be swept into crates and offered to a museum. There was a brief day of street theatre when one or two famously fogeyish writers joined a protest outside the shop. This manifestation of solidarity with superseded writing materials quickly fizzled out – though not before an abrasive, counter-revolutionary younger novelist had asked reporters in the street outside whether the next important battlefront to be opened up would be the defence of the quill pen.

The gold shimmer and fullness of that quill which enfolds the words ROBERTSON & SONS on the now dirty plate glass, catches Christopher's eye as he looks out into the sunlit street, where he notices a new diversion. Some great event is evidently taking place in the grey bunker, for hundreds of bald or grey-haired old men in suits with discreet lapel-pins are flooding out of it into the street. For an organisation once thought to be a secret sodality, they are remarkably conspicuous. What makes them wish to play this game of dressing-up? Why do they not look more cheerful as a result of this riot of elderly male comradeship? The normally quiet street is so choked with people that pedestrians are required to step smartly into the gutter in order to make their way down it without slackening speed.

He stretches out for his litre bottle of mineral water, allegedly captured from a Scottish spring, and dips his hand into a paper bag of soft ciabatta rolls filled with tuna and mayonnaise (these being the only ingredients he can identify with certainty). The day is becoming hotter and there is no sign of his absconding builders.

And so he succumbs to the stab of anxiety, of half-justified jealousy, of silent suffering.

~

Christopher considers that this was the first blow administered by Carmen, the first faltering of what they thought of – of what *he* thought of – as a love that would endure. He exaggerated. He had no hope of such a thing, no faith. The opportunist logicians of classic poetry – seize the day etc etc – were no doubt right. Gather the rosebuds while they are there to be gathered. Take it now. Outwit time. Those were the ground rules he had worked to before he met Carmen. Sometimes speciously, like those poets. Sometimes because he had come to believe it to be true (with partners who did not appear to dissent). But Carmen held out the possibility of something more. There had been nothing like it before, for him. He did not dare to speculate what the experience meant for her. She seemed to give so unstintingly of her self, to shame other people's day to day calculations, their reserve and holding back, their reluctance to let go. She gave all that she could, as if each hour existed for you to prove how much could be poured into it. And how much remained to flow, the barrel never empty.

What was she doing in Nice? Christopher tried to believe the offered version, that she was with an 'old friend'. Perhaps if he had listened a little more carefully to the gossip he would have heard of Jimmy's connection, that apartment which he rented out. But that would have been merely to bring nearer by a few weeks or months a reckoning that was inevitable. Now, of course, he had the full story but then he suffered in confusion and not knowing. It's hard not to fall in with the moralists, he reflected, and see this as the mandatory payback, the redemption of the mortgage deed, the punishment for pleasure.

During that first period apart – a week then seemed longer than seven days in duration – he slept badly. He would wake in the small hours and sometimes dress and walk out into the streets. There was always someone about, noise and drunken laughter, police sirens, smashing bottles. In Tottenham Court Road groups of whooping young girls, half-naked whatever the weather, high on alcohol and the lesser designer drugs and loud music and laughter, made their disorderly way home from clubs after the Tube had closed its gates. Bodies re-arranged themselves under blankets in doorways. Rubbish piled up outside the bars and restaurants. If Christopher were late enough he would see the bundles of newspapers being thrown out of vans outside newsagents' shops, hear the acceleration of traffic that had been subdued for only a couple of hours, sense the new day starting, its arrow pulled back against the string.

It was the not knowing that was the source of pain. Christopher and Carmen had declared often enough their mutual faith in freedom, in the refusal of petty restrictions. They claimed not to want to know about each other's activities, where these were of no necessary concern. They dreaded the life of the married couple (dread intensified by total ignorance) whom they supposed to be condemned to perpetual surveillance of each other's lives, rowing about the slightest tilt sideways of their nuptial bark, unable to act freely as individuals, always having to flaunt in the world's face the routines of the practised double act, always having to be seen to manage successfully the art of being The Couple.

We were not like that, Carmen, he whispers, but we foundered also. We had not discovered the secret of loving in perpetuity. You mocked me for even wanting such a thing. Perhaps you were right. You were the free spirit. Your giving was part of this. Knowing that the moment does not last, you threw yourself into transforming it, to exalting it, to making it sufficient of itself. And I shared in those episodes. I knew them. Is that not enough?

~

After Nice, after the self-dramatising coldness which they chose briefly as their substitute for the marital tiff, after the fortunate episode of Greece, they eventually found their balance again. The old passion resumed. Until the arrival of Carl. And through Carl, Joanna.

This time Christopher was responsible. Carl was an architect in charge of the Souper Kitchen chain's expansion programme. His job was to ensure that each new shop fitted exactly the specifications laid down in protocols drawn up in the Chicago head office of Souper Kitchen. Colour schemes, counter design, ratios of tables and chairs to floor space, size of neon signs, disposition of soup-urns, all had to be incorporated with exactitude into each new outlet. Chicago was adamant. There must be no deviation from the house-style. Carl threw himself into this task with the zeal of an officer of the Inquisition searching out every shade and nuance of individual heresy. His was the sort of mind that could not bear approximation, the fair-enough-that'll-do that is the working philosophy of the building trade. Christopher liked to think of him self as a perfectionist of sorts. He took pleasure and satisfaction in the skill with which he surmounted the usual obstacles: residual problems of space and size, wall angle, window position. But he was working always against the clock. And each client was different. Carl's client, by contrast, was always the same and the specification allowed for no individuation. Christopher would have found this frustrating but Carl approached his constraints with a sort of wild-eyed passion, derived extraordinary pleasure from them. It was exactly the impossibility of half-measures, the prohibition on almost getting it right, which animated him. Where Christopher might have quite enjoyed the inventive challenge of working around an immovable pipe, or an old fireplace which it had been decided to retain as an original feature, Carl would have taken this as a taunt, an affront. With a blaze of anger he would attack the obstruction which threatened to deflect the smooth implementation of his exact blueprint.

When Christopher first met Carl he was working on a Thai restaurant in Beak Street in Soho. Carl was next door, supervising the fitting-out of a new Souper Kitchen. Typically, these outlets fitted themselves into those narrow spaces once occupied by the small cafés which were rapidly disappearing from central London. Their trade was mostly soup to go for busy office workers with short lunch breaks. Seating inside was minimal. At the back of this particular shop (which was part of a long terraced building which the local authority had belatedly listed) was an odd marble remnant – probably eighteenth century in origin – which

Christopher guessed had originally been some sort of internal fountain in an inner court. The authorities, pending an archaeological investigation due to start in several months from the other side of the building, had decreed that the marble wall – about six metres in length – should remain. Three quarters of its length was in Christopher's restaurant and the rest protruded through to the old café where it had always been boxed in behind a false wall of tongue-and-groove boarding nailed to a framework of two-by-two. Christopher, for his part, was quite pleased to have found a solution: a long bench-seat resting on top of the marble which could be lifted up on a hinge if necessary for inspection. Carl, however, was not so easily satisfied. It was the howls of anger next door that drew his neighbour in to see what was the cause of the fracas.

Christopher found Carl surrounded by brick and sawdust, a metre-long aluminium spirit-level in his right hand which he held like the magic wand of a disconsolate Prospero measuring the ruin of his former dukedom. Around him – watchful, uncertain – stood two or three labourers. They had exhausted their usual repertoire of sarcasm, apparent inability to hear any instruction, sly disobedience, and muttered exasperation. None of this worked on Carl. He stood silently in his yellow hard-hat with orange brick-dust colouring his blond beard, staring at the short length of marble which offered its defiant rebuke to his dream of exact order. He was not ready to concede defeat. He would listen to no advice, no pragmatic reassurance. Christopher had heard something of this legendary perfectionist and it interested him to see Carl for the first time, to feel the pressure of his wordless anger that seemed so far in excess of the immediate provocation. It was a metaphysical condition.

And then Christopher began to offer his advice, sidling up to the question, asking for the plans, discovering (quite by accident, but Carl looked at him as if he were some saving messenger from the Gods) a potential loophole. The scheme devised by Chicago was posited on a fixed arrangement of elements whose disposition was apparently unalterable. It derived from exhaustive market research and was of a complexity that would have baffled a court functionary of the late Byzantine empire. Customer flows, 'decision-patterns', 'spend wishes', 'impulse triggers', had been precisely calibrated. The relationship between the desires of humans (who were accorded a freedom of action commensurate with the programmed reflexes of Pavlov's dog) and the arrangement of temptation (substantial item followed by lesser impulse purchase etc.), created in sum a web or subtle snare into which the customer would walk, inexorably. To place a rack of potato chips or a trough of fudge brownies in the wrong place would be to wreck the intricate dynamics worked out in computer simulations across the Atlantic. One false move and the entire precarious structure of controlled desire listed fatally.

But Christopher had spotted a chance of adaptation. The Water Bar, separated as it was from the purchasing nexus, and consisting of a large cool urn of plain tapwater for which there was no charge to the customer, had a weak relationship to the overall strategy. Hoping that the customer would purchase more expensive bottled mineral waters or juices, the Water Bar needed to be placed at the end of any counter-sequence. It was the place to which one went with a loaded tray when all the transactions were done. It was specified that it should go at the end of the line of arrayed goods. Christopher pointed out to Carl that the narrow shop was also quite short in length compared to many Souper Kitchens. The Water Bar might just fit according to specification but it would be tight. What if – he suggested – it were angled (admittedly a breach of the design principle of an unbroken straight line of temptation) so that it could be made to rest on a platform not unlike his bench-seat which would disguise the marble plinth.

Carl looked at him wordlessly, like someone surfacing from the deep, turbulent water of a dream. He stared at Christopher intently as if he were trying to gauge his motive. Was he a tempter, a sly Siren voice drawing him towards a perilous reef? Then he turned his head to look at the lump of marble embedded in the base of the wall. He looked down at the plans. There was a further period of silence. Christopher waited for him to make the next move in his own time. The alternating glances quickened. He shook the plans excitedly. He sighed deeply – this was the moment when he yielded to necessity, when he allowed that, at this time and in this place, there could not be realised an absolute perfection – and, with a noise like a swallowed grunt, he tore into his labourers, shouting and gesticulating, egging them on as if they, not he, had been the instrument of this agonising delay. They were pleased enough to get on with something, never having understood his peculiar intransigence in the first place, and they went to it with a will.

Later, when the fit was done, Carl came round to offer Christopher his thanks. He had his hard-hat in his hands and looked exhausted like an epic hero after battle. He sat on a crate in the middle of his new friend's restaurant floor, picking small wood-shavings from his ragged and holed jersey, taking occasional draughts from a bottle of water, and watching with approval the lime green panelling being hammered into position around the walls. He said that he did not care for Thai food but he knew a small restaurant nearby in Frith Street where he had proposed to take his wife (by way of compensation for a spate of late nights that had been needed to claw back the lost time occasioned by the difficulties in Beak Street). He asked if Christopher would like to join them. Something in the way he spoke of his wife and of the reasons for this outing alerted Christopher to a possible source of tension in the relationship. Having had his own difficulties with Carmen, he was reluctant to become involved just now as a spectator of marital dysfunction. He had always resented couples who seemed willing to inflict their private antagonisms on others, to rub their noses in it. (He and Carmen tried as far as they could to conduct their rows if not in private then away from the company of their friends.) But he found that he liked Carl. Perhaps Christopher thought that he represented the better side of him, the perfectionist he might have been had he cut fewer corners, accepted fewer Friday night jobs, agreed to fewer impossible deadlines. Christopher was still proud of his work but he knew that the fierce desire of Carl to get it absolutely right was now beyond him. He had stood at that turning, paused regretfully, then chosen the other fork in the road.

As it turned out his apprehensions had been wrong. Carl's wife, Joanna, was relaxed and warm. There was no bickering or shrillness or tight-lipped backchat between them – though Christopher sensed a certain scrupulously courteous indifference towards her on Carl's part. Joanna was, like all in the party, in her late thirties. She had very short black hair and was dressed in loose white linen which seemed to accentuate a certain delicate pallor in her complexion. Christopher watched Carmen looking her up and down, appraising her. It did not occur to him that she was assessing her as one might a potential rival. Carl and he talked a little shop until Carmen cut them short and drew the conversation on to more congenial subjects. The party was sitting, on this hot June evening, in the open, penned into a little enclosure on the pavement in front of the restaurant with a fine view of the comings and goings. Frith Street on these summer nights attracted crowds of lively, noisy people. Outside the pubs, large groups spilled on to the pavement, hugging their pint glasses to their bosoms, or swigging from chilled bottles. The men, Christopher noticed, always seemed to outnumber the women in these groups. At other cafés and bars and small restaurants, tables had been placed outside, as if, for these few weeks of tolerable weather, London was prepared to transform itself into a Mediterranean café society, in spite of its knowledge that the scope was brief and that the tables would eventually have to be stacked up and put away after a short exposure. Tourists and clubbers and idlers thronged the street. Cycle-taxis clustered in wait for trade at the junction with Old Compton Street. There was a queue outside Ronnie Scott's. Joanna, Christopher felt, was a little detached from everyone else and the conversation. Her attention was taken by the people on the street. He was just about to wave away a rose-seller when Joanna stopped him and took a small bunch, crushed into cellophane, from the Balkan woman who carried them in a quiver in the crook of her arm. She laid the flowers on her white lap and it suddenly struck him how beautiful she looked. Carl and Carmen had locked horns over some movie about which they disagreed violently and were ignoring them. Christopher smiled at Joanna.

I was wrong, Carmen, he considers. I was so ready to blame you but I too was culpable. I used your willingness to go your own way as a permit for my own adventure but I paid a price which I now regret. There was no love like yours (I want you to think this too, wherever you might be) and I squandered the advantage. That was the mistake we both made. We tore up the title deed to our mutual happiness and scattered the pieces in the wind. It is for this reason that I lie alone here, listening to the dull traffic hum, the shouts in the street, wondering what has become of the free spirit I once thought myself to be. It is why I struggle to recoup the lost memories of our time together, remembering, painfully, what I so carelessly threw away.

A week later, coming down Windmill Street with some brass hinges that he had just collected for a job from Windmill Tools and Hardware, Christopher saw Joanna as she tripped out of a small gallery. She was the first to wave. He suggested coffee. They talked, laughed, found a chance to discover some common ground that their brief outdoor meal had not quite allowed them to establish, and parted easily. He thought, for both of them, that was an end of it. And then, unsurprisingly, for she and Carl rented a mansion flat near Gower Street, he began to meet her – accidentally but quite frequently – in the little streets of Fitzrovia and Soho where most of his work was to be found. Often, potential clients would walk into a place where he was working and ask for his card. In this way he did not have to look for work elsewhere in the capital. He and Joanna mostly contented themselves with a quick coffee, because he did not have much time to spare, but once or twice, when he was between jobs or waiting for some sub-contractors to complete a component of the refit, he was free for lunch. The summer continued to bathe everything in a rather steamy heat. His eyes would sting with what he assumed to be pollution. There was a smell of traffic fumes in the air but also, at times, a pleasant languour, tables in the sun, glasses of chilled wine, a sense of some recovered ease, the memory of past summers, lost summers, no doubt imaginary summers, when one could allow oneself a little respite from the demands of the clock and the diary, the peremptory present. Perhaps it was this that lowered his guard, he reflects, that allowed him to forget Carmen for a moment. A moment that proved fateful.

Perhaps she might not have gone back again to Jimmy – or with such consequences – had he been more attentive, had he not wandered during those few weeks in the city sun. He wants, now, to seek a reason, to make it logical, to suppress the idea that what happened was without reason or necessity or pattern. He wants an explanation but he has none.

Jimmy interrogates himself: did I feel guilty about my role in wrecking the relationship of these two people? Should the hateful Jimmy dress himself in penitential costume and beg forgiveness? But whose forgiveness, and for what misdemeanour precisely? I was hardly, in this instance, an odious seducer, spotting his opportunity like a soaring hawk who plummets to earth to clamp his talons on the soft neck of a helpless prey. Carmen came to me freely. No, no, you will not hear me say "threw herself at me" – that is certainly the language of the professional predator.

Jimmy struggles to recollect the beginning of his amatory narrative. It begins, he considers, in a series of casual encounters. A small concert at the Wigmore one bright autumn Sunday lunchtime. A supper party in Holland Park thrown by some theatrical people, which turned out to have the flavour of a business meeting, a public relations initiative. A private view. The opening of a ghastly new Mediterranean restaurant somewhere near the British Museum. Christopher, whom he always referred to with unfeeling sarcasm as The Gentleman Builder, may, he reflected, have had a hand in the design of that place.

Perhaps it was the memory of the sort of restaurant preferred by his father, who would ritually take him out for Sunday lunch on the first day of the school holidays to some old-fashioned place characterised by gilt mirrors, heavy silver tableware, antique yet courteous waiters (Jimmy had never understood the new fashion for rudeness) and understated menus, that had prevented his delighting in these instantly-refitted, over-designed, noisy bistros. No matter which European capital they were settled in at the time, his father would find his way to these older places. There was one in Rome with a mosaic floor in the entrance lobby representing a school of dolphin which he could see now was probably a copy of some Roman original and therefore culpable of its own kind of vulgarity, but he was always struck by the great calm of these establishments. Perhaps that was their function: to celebrate a world of settled assurance where the rich and cultivated could move in the knowledge that this was an experience to which they were both accustomed and entitled. He could quite see how, early in the course of a people's revolution, such places would be singled out for storming.

Jimmy was introduced to the concept of guilt by his Jesuit teachers (the family arrived in Rome just at the point when he was ready for secondary education and his father, forgetting the ancient faith of his family, chose the Academia San Vicenzo on grounds which Jimmy suspected were purely aesthetic: the school was located in a delightful ochre building next to a church whose cloisters surrounded a beautifully tended garden). It is probably inadvisable to expose small boys to the notion of guilt. They will immediately proceed to take it too much to heart. Nor is it an especially useful mental condition. For not merely does it have little or no effect in halting any misdemeanour, it both saddles those who were prepared to do wrong anyway with an unnecessary burden, and perpetuates the notion that we are governed by a subtle moral order of repentance and remorse – when in fact we are usually guided by our instinctive drives alone. In a happy phrase, Carmen called Jimmy a "moral Macchiavelli". This he interpreted as an attempt to pass the responsibility for what was happening entirely to him, and, as usual, he acquiesced.

Jimmy's manner (which was derived from his comfortable, guilt-free cosmopolitan inheritance) never wholly ceased to annoy Carmen. He could seem too languid for her taste, too untroubled. She was, like most of her contemporaries, a driven thing. She lived in a constant race of activity, as if she feared to stand still. Both work (which figured more prominently in her life than he thought wise) and leisure seemed conducted in a panic. She was also intensely combative. Jimmy had been told many times by mutual friends of her legendary rows with her partner. He considered that this was part of the same need: to confront and to face down and by thus asserting oneself to make oneself aware of one's pulsating energies. I argue, therefore I am. Only those who are deeply assured can afford to be careless of whether they succeed or fail in social contests. After the first rehearsal in Nice they argued about this constantly. She felt that he was insufficiently aware of the struggle that had been enforced on her by her working-class background. No doubt tactlessly, he pointed out that her period of struggle had been remarkably short-lived and had by now been eclipsed by the period of her success. She was magnificently scornful. Nothing Jimmy could do or say would redeem him in her eyes. He was the lazy toff, softened by a lifetime without struggle or material anxiety. He made some lame attempts to describe the difficulties of his early musical career which had been marked by failures, by a long effort to make his mark (not helped by his preference for the innovative and the avant-garde) but she simply would not accept this plea in mitigation. The quality of her grievance was of a purity and an intensity that brooked no comparison. She trilled the refrain that he had heard from so many beautiful heroines: "You do not understand."

But, yes, Jimmy now admits to himself, I was guilty. I should have intuited that our relationship would not work. That, far from its being the result of the sly and sophisticated manipulations of this moral *Principe*, it was embarked on by her in order to counteract the difficulties she was having with The Gentleman Builder. What these were I never quite divined but other people's relationships are a subject, I have generally found, best avoided. I can see now that I should have extricated myself far earlier. I should have rebuffed her, perhaps, before our affair ever began. But (I am late coming to this) she was to me utterly desirable. I could not resist her. I could not turn her away. My reasoning was not Jesuitical but visceral. I wanted her because of what she was, because of what she awoke in me, and our superficial arguments and ratiocinations hardly bore on the case. Yes, I plead guilty, as when, after a long drawn out avoidance, I owned up to a minor offence (a window broken by a thrown football boot in the communal shower room during some high jinks) and the tall, lean priest with the steel-rimmed glasses gloated in triumph when I delivered myself to him. He turned it into a moral seminar, refusing to beat me, forcing me to analyse what I had done, to take pride in my courage in accepting blame, to trace the refinements of conscience, the personal sequence of decisions and actions that had flowed from that silent self-examination. Yes, yes, I plead guilty.

But that incident on the coast-road beyond Menton (so sudden and violent that it struck me like an intended reprimand from some unseen and supernatural moral being) changed everything. We were united, complicit in that horror, in our responsibility for it. Her first reaction was to flee. I gather that she went back to her partner, that they went abroad and found some solace 'on the rebound' as her magazine relationship-dissectors would put it. But she came back. I accepted her back, as if there were unfinished business that we needed to see through to a conclusion. It was unsatisfactory and intermittent. I gather also that her partner became involved, briefly, with someone else. The pattern became more complicated. I cannot say whether the shock of the child's death disoriented us all, drew in, one by one, these other actors, or whether what happened was the result of our common instability – rootless, untethered people following only the logic of our desires. But what other logic leads us forwards?

Their first meeting after Nice, which he eventually allowed to have taken place, was at the launch of a book of photographs taken by an acquaintance of Carmen's, Ben Bush. This event took place in a small gallery in East London and the evidence of Ben's talent was arrayed on its freshly-rollered white walls. The photographs in the book were of contemporary street-people – homeless, derelict, impoverished drug-users. His art seemed to make these people look even more desperate than they must have appeared in real life. They stood out starkly in shadowed landscapes, like etchings of figures in a mediaeval hell. Jimmy felt that the images were too beautiful, that their art imposed a barrier between him and the quality of real suffering that their subjects had patently undergone. The heat of the crowded gallery drove him out into a small paved yard at the back of the gallery where, in spite of the late sunshine, it was gratifyingly cool in contrast to the inner inferno. As he passed towards the brick wall at the bottom of the yard (topped with ugly razor wire) he heard a shout behind him.

"Jimmy!"

"Carmen, I didn't expect to see you here."

All his desire, his helplessness before Carmen's presence rushed back to him. He wanted her again and he struggled to think of some diverting strategy. He told her of his reservations about the photographs and she ripped into him with vigour. He stood accused of aesthetic naïveté, of failure to understand the relationship between treatment and subject, and much else. He took his drubbing with a smile, feasting on her animation, the splendour of her invective. She was on magnificent form. Christopher came over to join them. Had he known of Jimmy's recent role in Carmen's life, the musician felt sure that it would have been evident in his manner – in certain emphatic ironies, or waspish interventions, a mocking tolerance. But it was clear that he had, at this stage, no idea that Jimmy was the bounder and cad who had seduced his lover away from him. Jimmy guessed that Carmen had been vague about Nice. She was very good at withholding any information which she considered it unnecessary for others to know. Christopher's frank cordiality of manner and general air of ease in Jimmy's presence confirmed to him that she had not come clean with him. At their last meeting the two men had got off on the wrong foot after Christopher had made some crass observation about a Mark Anthony Turnage piece he had just recorded. Nothing endeared him less to the English than the boundless self-confidence with which, it seemed to him, they flaunted their aesthetic conservatism, not content to display it but seeking at the same time to compel one's approval of it, and his anger on that occasion had no doubt resulted in a lack of sophistication in rebuttal. But if Christopher had resented that righteous anger there was no sign of difficulty in his manner.

"Jimmy, you've met Christopher haven't you?"

"Yes, wasn't it at that restaurant-opening in Museum Street? What was that place called?"

"Kerkyra."

"That's it. And didn't you have a hand in the décor, Christopher?"

"I did. I remember that one very vividly. We were still working on it two hours before everyone sat down."

"I don't know how you can work at such speed. I seem to be getting slower and slower. It takes me a week these days to read a score properly and get myself into a position to start working on an interpretation."

Carmen took a rapid glug of her Chardonnay and launched delightedly into the attack.

"That's fine for the idle rich, but the rest of us have to move faster and faster these days just to stand still."

"I rather object to the term idle."

Christopher agreed with Jimmy.

"Jimmy's right. He doesn't sound very idle to me. Haven't you just got back from Paris?"

As Jimmy nodded, Carmen looked at him sharply as if his presence in Paris were somehow further evidence of his failure to pay proper homage to the deities of work.

"It's just a phrase. Jimmy knows what I mean. We've argued about this before. He thinks the lower orders protest too much. We aren't quite insouciant enough for him."

"Carmen, you are trying to wind me up. But I am too full of this excellent wine to be rattled. You just hammer away and I'll smile sweetly at whatever you say. That's sure to drive you so mad that you'll go back into that inferno and start an argument with someone else."

In fact it was Christopher who started back to the door at this point. He had spotted someone he knew and therefore excused himself. Left alone with Carmen, Jimmy could hardly contain myself. He wanted her, there and then, and to hell with all these trappings of urbane irony and word-play.

"I gather you were in Paris at the same time as Alice," she said with twinkling malice.

Jimmy resolved to meet her glittering provocation with an affectation of unruffled coolness.

"Yes, we had lunch. She seems on good form. Did you know she was about to throw it all in?"

"Yes, she told me."

Not liking the tone of this exchange he decided that two could be provocative.

"She was looking stunning."

"Alice always does. It's Alice's thing."

"I took her to a place my father was very fond of. It hasn't changed in thirty years."

"I find those places so dreary. I like change. I like innovation. Why should a restaurant be like a mausoleum?"

"I doubt if one would eat so well in a mausoleum."

"Yes, but what about all those half-dead *bourgeois* relics with their spotted skin and expensive jewellery and fussy demands."

"There were a few of those, I agree, but Alice caught sight of one of her celebrity chums – you know the actress Selena Seferis? Well, she's hardly half-dead, is she?"

"Oh, these *nouveaux riches* love to play with such places. They think they are anointing them with the sacred water of celebrity and cool. Like Mick Jagger buying a Jacobean manor house in Somerset. I suppose she got up half way through her meal to snort some cocaine in the Ladies."

"Possibly. But aren't we being a little bitchy this evening?"

"Jimmy, why do you use these expressions?"

"Oh, no doubt because of my linguistic impoverishment. You must teach me some new vocabulary."

There was a pause. Jimmy thought Carmen was about to say something but she checked herself. He knew that she wanted to know what had happened between Alice and himself, whether, for example, lunch was followed by any other intimacy, but she was too proud even to be seen to be fishing for answers to her unvoiced questions. He took no pleasure in tantalising her but equally he had no wish to be put in the dock. Then she suddenly put out her arm and touched his forearm lightly. Her hand rested there briefly. He could smell her scent. He could sense the tension in her body. Her desire. The power of this unspoken feeling silenced both of them. The wrong words could have wrecked this moment so they chose to use none.

She had withdrawn her hand before Christopher returned, with a red-faced type in tow in a grubby white jacket, dirty trainers on his feet. Hanks of stringy and disordered hair had been scraped across the bald summit of his scalp. His glass was slopping over and he was waving his arms about. Ignoring Carmen's scowl of disapproval, he insisted on introducing himself.

"Peter Worsley. Christopher was telling me you interviewed Lavinia Watersmith not so long ago. I had her on *The Culture* a couple of years ago but I am sure we haven't milked her dry yet. I am quite keen to set up an interview to coincide with the Francis Quine exhibition at the Tate. You've got to catch these old biddies before they croak. They always give good value for money."

"Why's that?" Jimmy found himself asking rather tartly.

He was familiar with Worsley, who had interviewed him on his weekly radio arts programme a year earlier. It purported to be a discussion about the public's tolerance of new music but it turned out to be the usual ritual display of soundbites provided by a round-up of people who seemed to Jimmy to have little passion for music of any kind. He was cast as the Uncompromising Artist, and round the studio table there was an Earnest Provincial Post-Modernist Academic, a Smirking Populist, and a New Labour Voice Machine. Worsley slurped his way through two bottles of wine, occasionally sending the bottle in the direction of the panel as an afterthought, before abruptly calling time in response to a gesture from the producer on the other side of the soundproof glass who mimed the slashing of his own throat – a gesture with which Jimmy could only sympathise.

"Well, first of all they do Posh. Those high-pitched

upper crust voices talking about Bertie and Virginia and Aldous are cracking radio. And then there's the sheer bloody marvel that they're still alive. Still churning out anecdotes about people whom you thought had died half a century ago – at least. The market for this sort of thing is always buoyant."

"But you aren't really talking about the artistic giants are you? These people were minor players even in their own day."

"True but the big game have all been bagged."

Carmen now cut in aggressively. "How do you rate Ben Bush then?"

She gestured towards the photographer, who was now out in the yard like every other escapee from the heat of the gallery and surrounded by admirers. He was dressed in black with Ray-Bans propped up on the top of his head. He rolled a cigarette, while a blonde journalist with a small Sony recorded his clipped replies to her questions.

"Don't care for his stuff much. It's all been done better by Danziger. But he's very sexy just now. *The Observer* are doing a feature on Sunday. The book is in the hardback top ten. We can't afford to ignore it."

"What is the radio equivalent of bums on seats?" Christopher suddenly asked.

"Earholes on static," suggested Carmen with a laugh.

Worsley looked a little put out. He probably thought that they weren't taking him seriously enough. In common with most people in his trade he had an immoveable conviction of his own importance but at the same time required periodic affirmation of that status. Like someone pressing a safety button he signalled madly to another group and, making a swift apology, darted off to join them. They all looked at each other in relief. Christopher spoke first.

"It's faintly worrying that people like that are in charge

of the imaginary museum."

"I have never met anyone who actually listens to his programme," said Carmen.

"Oh I am sure there are a few insomniacs, lonely car drivers, academics wondering how to break in to the racket," Jimmy speculated. "It's just as well that the listeners can't see him, given his standards of personal grooming."

Carmen now indicated that she had had enough. Christopher nodded his agreement but first she dashed across to Bush, cutting across his interviewer, and pecked him on the cheek, then muttered some non-specific approbation about the show. Jimmy watched her go, thinking that he too must follow. But, when she reached the open door of the gallery, she turned, in the realisation that she had left behind a tote-bag of papers on a table placed against the rear wall of the yard. She walked quickly back towards Jimmy. He watched every motion of her body and when she came up to him he knew that she had been aware of the greed of his gaze. She bent to pick up the bag and said, quickly, in a matter-of-fact tone: "Jimmy, give me a call. I've got to go now."

His eyes followed her again as she retraced her way across the yard. Christopher was waiting to gather her into the care of his outstretched arm. He turned to Jimmy and smiled in all candour. Then they both disappeared.

Jimmy waited for a few minutes, walked back into the gallery to take another look at the photographs, then slipped quietly away, knowing that he would indeed ring Carmen, very probably the next day.

Carmen knew that she should not have gone back to Jimmy. After Nice something had changed in her, quite apart from the particular change in the way she saw him. There was now something unpleasant, reproachful, quite hideous, in their mutual history. She knew that the right thing would have been to cut him out of her life, to concentrate either on rebuilding her relationship with Christopher or on the task of finding a new direction. That had always been her response to any personal crisis or dilemma: to move on. She loathed therapies, analyses, probes, and inquests. She wanted always to snatch a new beginning from the ruins of the present moment. She wanted to act. Perhaps this was naive, to think that one can cut loose, that one can cancel out the memory of failure. Might it not come back, inevitably, to haunt one? Or was that to concede too much to the memory-merchants, the exactors of retribution, the people who do not want to see you go, slipping out of their hands? She had always wanted to be free and had been perplexed throughout her life at how this ruling desire is not widespread, at how passionately so many love their slavery.

Carmen went back to Jimmy. He rang her on the morning after the private view. She could hear music playing in the background which surprised her, for he would always lecture her about combining music with other activities. He saw this as a demonstration that one was not listening. He sounded a little distracted, a little uncertain, as if he knew, as she did, that this was unwise, that the proper path was well understood and that they were choosing not to take it. They agreed to meet for lunch at a little place in Dean Street of which thay had been fond. The choice seemed to suggest a touch of harmless nostalgia: two old friends meeting again for old time's sake. To have chosen a new venue would have been too much like a bold step forward into new terrain. When the manager came from the rear of the restaurant, recognised them, greeted them warmly, they both experienced a tremor of unease. Like guilty lovers, terrified at being found out, uneasy at their momentary triumphs, they smiled nervously at the manager, accepted the menu cards – and laughed when Jimmy, without thinking, ordered a particular Muscadet. This had always been their way of starting a meal on the first, rare and intermittent, summer evenings they spent together, while Christopher toiled late at some overdue refit, in the weeks before Nice.

They drank their wine, ordered, broke their bread rolls, and drank their chilled soup accompanied by a steady murmur of unexcitable conversation. They moved these banalities between them like counters on a board. Neither seemed willing, at first, to raise the stakes, to say what needed to be said. Carmen decided that she had better start to force the pace.

"So Alice is giving it all up. Did she tell you why?"

"Not really. I assumed that she wanted to quit while she was ahead. Her assets are not renewable, sadly."

"But she's still in good shape."

"Well, you've seen her recently yourself."

"Did she talk about that."

"Not really. I take it she told you more than she told me."

"I think that there might have been some... catalyst but I think her official reasons are sensible enough."

"She seems very astute. She has invested very wisely in

property in various cities. I don't think she will have to struggle. And if the book dishes the right amount of dirt she should do very well out of it."

"Do you like Alice?"

"Yes."

"You seem to hesitate."

"I suppose I do. There is a sort of controlling element in her which makes me uneasy."

"I thought you found me too bossy as well."

"No, it's not that. I don't mind boisterous, combative people who fight their corner. This is something else. It's a kind of awesome self-control that I find quite chilling. It's hard to express it but I find her too perfect. The looks are part of it and since they are her professional tools, as it were, she has to work on them, keep them well-oiled and sharpened. I can't criticise her for that. No, I suppose it's the way everything fits so neatly. Her diary, her movements from one flat to the other, one city to another, her routine in the gym. I don't know how she conducts her love-life but I am sure it is equally well-regulated. There isn't a lot left to chance in Alice's life."

"You didn't discuss her love-life, garner any personal insights?"

"Carmen, that's rather low-level sarcasm for you."

"I was wondering what you two did in Paris."

"Why don't you just come out with it. Did I sleep with Alice? No I didn't sleep with Alice. OK?"

"OK. Sorry, I shouldn't have asked."

Jimmy put his hand over hers, he picked a tiny bread-crumb off her sleeve with his free hand and they said nothing for a few moments. Carmen knew she was playing with fire but what could she do? After the meal they went back to his apartment near Regent's Park. It was all so easy. Inevitable.

Looking back, Carmen told herself that she wouldn't have blamed Christopher – had he known the full facts – for taking the same liberty. But the fact is, knowing that he was unaware of Jimmy's presence in her life, she did indeed blame him. She had no right but she blamed him nonetheless. She was not proud of that. She frankly owned to being a monstrous hypocrite. During one of their rows she even managed to tell Christopher that it was because she loved him that she was hurt by his betrayal. Yet still she wouldn't tell him about Jimmy. He had to learn that for himself from other people, from guesswork, from hints. She never told him about Nice. It had become too complex a memory for her. She wasn't suppressing it but every time her mind settled on it the implications became more distasteful. Later, she discovered that Jimmy saw it as some sort of sign, a celestial rebuke for their misbehaviour. She told him that this was a mere hang-up from his Jesuitical education, that they were living in the twenty-first century, that the Gods had departed. Once again, she was talking herself up, trying to silence the voice in her head, the one that said the same thing in a different touchy-feely version. She would conclude that you can't escape the notion that your actions have consequences, whatever mythological, theological, therapeutic babble you use to express the thought. What unsettled her about the death of that child was the fact that she couldn't separate out the idea of culpability (were they, in the end, responsible; could it have been avoided?) from all the other reasons to be guilty that paraded before the ethical camera-eye.

Sometimes she looked back to her schooldays, to what people think of as the simple pieties of the nuns. In her twenties she repudiated the lot. She laughed at what seemed their platitudinous banality but later she came to see it differently. She began to see that even the most clumsy attempt at plotting a moral course may be an attempt worth the effort. She felt, rightly or wrongly, that the nuns were out of their depth, professionally required to deal in certain concepts that their platitudes simply reduced, ossified, stripped of the vital dimension of life and growth, the tension of individual choice. The world offered its challenges beyond the brick wall and cast iron railing perimeter of their convent in the suburbs. The only tools that would prove adequate to that challenge were the ones that could tackle any sort of mess. Today, in her thirties, she was no longer certain even of her repudiations. She had passed into a new phase where she was not sure what she believed. She suspected this to be, at present, a more or less universal condition.

Christopher knew something had happened in Nice but with her second dalliance he came to know more or less everything. That he hated Jimmy was obvious enough. Men, Carmen considered, do not always react like this. Sometimes they become oddly magnanimous and forgiving. She had always put this down to their own secret guilts but now she wondered if there were not something more intricate and puzzling to this way of reacting than she could comprehend. Christopher's contempt for Jimmy was absolute. So ferocious indeed that it ended by more or less letting her off the hook. She was uncomfortable with this for she knew she was no saint. She felt sorry for Christopher, genuinely sorry, for she knew that he loved her with an intensity that was new for her, that she had never known in any previous relationship. She felt certain that he also had never known it.

Perhaps, too, she felt sorry for both of them, for the melancholy wreck of their life together, for the imbecile way in which they had thrown away their love.

But then Joanna came on to the scene. From the moment

Carmen saw her she sensed trouble. She immediately developed towards her a powerful animosity. This was her first mistake because it awoke Christopher's sense of fair play. It was as if he needed to protect Joanna from her – which was absurd to begin with and then, of course, inevitable. Carmen knew that she was in a weak position but could not find a way to be consistent. I am a human being after all, she protested. At her first meeting with Joanna at the restaurant where they were the guests of her husband, Carl, she found the man decent enough but something of a bore. The amount of information she could take on board about industrial flooring and ceramic tiles was severely limited and on this occasion – to do with Christopher's having rescued him from that design dilemma – there was more of it than could be considered decent. Although she had never been much disposed to girl's chat, Carmen could have taken refuge in talking to Joanna, but her hostility was already being cranked up and they didn't get very far. Carl was a well-built, handsome guy with untidy blond hair and rather large, rough hands which his trade had made rougher. Although he was an architect, he seemed so obsessive that his work was invariably 'hands-on'. He would discard his management suit jacket and get down with the men, wrestling with the sheer physicality of the task in front of him. There was a stark, blue glitter in his eye which ought to have been seductive in a challenging sort of way but which, as the evening wore on, Carmen discovered to be the light of mania. In fact, she thought, he was barking. What sort of life was it to prowl the streets of central London looking for opportunities to force a dreary template onto various recalcitrant premises? He seemed to have no other life, no hinterland of interests or passions outside this obsessive Procrustean job of work. No interest, that is, except large and expensive cars. She nearly wept when the conversation, having finally wrung the last drop from the matter of cutting-edge German floor varnish, modulated easily into a discussion of the new range of Audis. No subject could have been better designed to send her into a sullen and subdued rage than that of motoring. She called for another bottle of wine, threw out some outrageous provocations – to no avail – then resigned herself to some occasional sarcasms and listless (but doomed) attempts to prod Joanna into life. Living in Whitfield Street, she walked everywhere that was possibly of interest and there was always a taxi available should she ever find herself in some barbarian outpost (a provincial main-line railway station, the end of the District Line, Wood Green after midnight). The car was simply a thing that did not intrude on her consciousness if she could help it.

When they finally reached the end of this exasperating evening; when Carl had kissed her on both cheeks; and when Christopher had done the same to the simpering Joanna, who now clutched a spray of roses which she had persuaded Chrisopher to offer her, a tribute he would not have been so foolish as to try to pay Carmen. As they walked through the busy streets of Soho, Carmen and Christopher were squaring up for a major argument. Having drunk too much, in order to soothe the ache of her boredom, she was louder and coarser than she would have wished to be. Christopher – already smitten by the pale rose girl? – was quiet and restrained, less disposed than usual to rise to her challenges and poisoned darts.

"I think I now know all I am ever likely to need to know about the art of laying wooden flooring."

"You have to realise that Carl is a perfectionist."

"Don't you mean a bore and a tyrant?"

"He cares about his work. It's his life."

"My point exactly. What sort of a life is it that turns on whether a millimetre needs to be shaved off a Spanish tile?

The man is an automaton. He's only half alive."

"Sometimes I think you don't appreciate that other people have different ways of taking their satisfactions in life."

"Oh, don't get me wrong. I know it all too well. But generally I stay well out of their way. Life is too short to spend it in the company of bores."

"I thought Joanna was quite pleasant."

"Quite pleasant! Do me a favour! She hardly said a thing all night, sitting there with those fucking roses in her lap like a virgin bridesmaid."

"I think that's a bit unfair."

"Oh, I'm sorry if I was unfair. That was quite wrong of me. Perish the thought that anyone should be unfair. She was more your type was she? The pale English rose?"

"Save your clichés for your magazine pieces."

"So what was the appeal, then? Grown tired of loud-mouthed bitches?"

"Since you mention it, you were a bit over the top tonight."

"Over the top! Look, I was fighting for my life out there. Trapped between two megabores locked into the intricacies of fucking varnish and Miss Muffet and her floral arrange-ment, I was trying to inject some spark into that heap of sawdust. And to cap it all you then launch into a discussion of motor cars! You don't even own one."

"You must provide me, next time, with a list of approved topics of conversation."

"Chris my sweet, there won't be a next time. If you and Carl want to salivate over gearboxes do it sometime when I'm out of town."

Their conversation had become so animated that Carmen hardly noticed her surroundings. She nearly trod on a beggar who was holding out a paper cup at his pitch under an ATM in Oxford Street. He looked at her with pained disapproval.

"Have a nice day."

"Chance would be a fine thing."

As if to rebuke her, Christopher walked firmly over to the young man and placed a couple of pound coins in his cup, which bore the livery of Souper Kitchen.

They carried on, the argument declining in ever-decreasing circles until it ended in mere coarse invective. And then in silence. Next day Carmen had to fly to Malaga to cover a travel-trade conference for one of her bread-and-butter magazines and she left early. Christopher was still asleep. It turned out to be a busy assignment and she met a few people whom she had not seen for some time so she soon forgot that tedious meal and their row (which, she knew, was not out of the ordinary). Later, she wondered if it was that very day that aggrieved Christopher first picked up the phone to Joanna, suggesting an innocent enough meeting, a pleasant lunch on a sunny London pavement. Everything about Joanna was pleasant. The word summed her up. No greater contrast than with herself: motormouth, the hard bitch, the tough cookie. Definitely not pleasant.

Yet, that is not how I see myself, she now thinks. I do not believe it was how Christopher truly saw me. Our sparring and shouting was a kind of playful ritual, a letting-off of steam, a declaration of our energy and passion, a proof – I always felt – that we were alive. He opened me up, he taught me that I could give and I believe that I gave him a great deal. I loved him. I still love him. But we have cast each other adrift. We have destroyed our own happiness. Today, I do not even know where I could begin to find him.

Throughout that summer Christopher's meetings with Joanna increased in frequency. Carmen's reactions had amused him. There was something about Joanna 'the English rose' that riled her. Her own noisy, feisty, energetic style of handling people could not be further removed from Joanna's delicate quietness. Joanna's meetings with Christopher were always brief – he was absconding from jobs where he was needed and to which it was always necessary that he return after an hour or two at most. But he appreciated their encounters all the more for their calming effect. This was how it was for the first weeks. No thought of anything other than pleasant conversation at outdoor tables in the bright mid-morning sunshine. Joanna was a girl from the Surrey suburbs, pretty but rather anxious, as if she were shouldering some great burden, as though she were, in some way Christopher could never manage to define, up against it. The world troubled and harassed her but the concerns which she admitted to him seemed deeply trivial. She rose above them. She triumphed. She shook out her hair with the air of someone who was not going to be defeated by what life threw at her. She smiled a wry, gentle smile of courageous acceptance. Christopher reflected that he had known so many of these girls. He pitied them but he never quite managed to under-stand the fardels that they seem to bear.

Christopher was puzzled by her marriage to Carl. With his moody silences and wordless obsessiveness, his lack of any evident polish or *savoir-faire* in social intercourse, he seemed altogether too coarse for the young woman he watched across those café tables. Christopher did not pry but he could sense that this was a marriage made in haste and now being repented of with extreme tentativeness. She would have been happier, he thought, with a long garden hedged by privet, green gloves and a trug, tut-tutting over rose-blight and the devastation wrought by slugs. Instead she was the chatelaine of a four-bedroomed mansion flat off Gower Street a stone's throw from Heal's. When Christopher eventually entered it he had to admire her skill in furnishing and decorating the surprisingly large space. Skills handed on to her by her mother had been extended by the apartment's challenges. She had struck a balance between the traditional reassurances of *bourgeois* taste and forays into the contemporary. He was particularly struck by the art works that hung on the walls. To his surprise, she pointed out a competent oil of the bookstalls on the Left Bank, with ripples of light on the Seine: "That was done by Carl."

Later, much later, after they had made love one after-noon in one of the spare bedrooms, when they both felt they had gone too far but had lost the means to retrace their steps, Joanna sat up and scanned the walls and ceilings of the room as if she were trying to find some defect in the furnishings or decoration as if this would point a way forward for her, untie this tangle of crossed paths into which she had allowed herself to be drawn.

Christopher did not know what she saw in him. Perhaps it was simply his availability, his proximity. His time was sufficiently scarce that he did not threaten to overwhelm her with his attention. He would not swamp her. For his part he did not have the inclination to put a stop to the affair (for he knew that it would end in its own way, prob-ably very soon, for it was not built to last). He was being used, no doubt, but in such cases it is not always easy to tell the user from the used. He was angry with Carmen and filled with jealousy and suspicion, feelings which he used to justify this betrayal. Christopher and Joanna were both haunted by the shadow of absent partners – like people who have begun a dinner party where the principal guests have not arrived. It was not a happy episode and Christopher soon found himself wanting it to end, regretting that it had not remained as a series of pleasant encounters in the sun.

In those early meetings Joanna would ask Christopher about Carmen, not being in the slightest degree aware of the latter's hostility towards her. Not having any career of her own other than homemaker (he later discovered that she was attending daytime lectures in the history of art for a diploma of some kind) she had evidently spent her life pumping people who had real jobs for details of what they did. "Is she compiling a careers directory?" Carmen had spat out venomously during one of the rows. Joanna seemed surprised and a little put out when Christopher explained Carmen's attitude to her work. Joanna found it difficult to understand that peculiar combination of brilliant performance and self-contempt that was the career of Carmen. Why would anyone persist in a way of earning one's living that was so much despised?

"She's very... trenchant, isn't she?" Joanna ventured one day as she sat with Christopher in a sunlit corner of the Café Rossignol in Berwick Street. He laughed and Joanna seemed rather hurt. He assured her that he was not mocking her but that Carmen's trenchancy was her signature, her way of being alive.

"I wonder what sort of childhood she had. That's often the key, isn't it? Was she an only child?"

"I think she was. But I can't be sure. She never talks about things like that. If she were an only child it would probably be just as well. I can't imagine how any rival would have fared. Because any sibling would immediately have been identified as a rival."

"Is she very competitive?"

"You'd have to ask her that yourself. In a way, I suppose. She likes to have arguments and then win them. She's not a good loser."

"I had a brother, three years older than me."

"Had?"

"Yes, he died on a climbing expedition. They shouldn't have gone. It was all so unnecessary. It was horrible. The teacher who took them eventually committed suicide. But it seems as though it wasn't really his fault. All so unnecessary."

Christopher waited for Joanna to collect herself after this tearful (as it became) recital. There was a quality of innocence about her, a childlike plainness of seeing and speaking, that touched him, accustomed as he was to hard-boiled grapples with Carmen and her circle. Perhaps, he considered, this was his contribution to the slide towards intimacy: a sort of pity for the poor girl (who of course wasn't a girl at all), a need to offer protection. Pity also for her evident need for affection, for some tenderness from the oaf, Carl, whose finer feelings (notwithstanding his youthful daubs) seemed reserved for walnut dashboards and the art of the carburettor. No doubt this is how all such affairs begin. In a flurry of specious logic.

And there was the case of Jimmy.

Christopher now began to suspect that Jimmy may have been involved – in some fashion he couldn't pinpoint – in the now notorious trip to Nice. At any rate, he discovered, in the usual grubby, piecemeal, lowering way, from friends and acquaintances and the putting together of two and two, that Jimmy was very much in the present frame. Christopher began, as one usually does, by blaming himself, the simplest and most unthinking strategy. He had neglected her for his work. He had not been around. He had maddened her into rows that perhaps could have been avoided. He had not, perhaps, given her enough, recognised the signals she was sending him, learned to accept the gifts she was prepared to lavish on him.

I know now, Carmen, Christopher rebuked himself. Now that I have lost you. I am now the scrupulous accountant of loss. I see it all with absolute clarity. How perfect is the vision afforded by impotent remorse! In the days of my present dissipation I at last get the message. (He sold the Whitfield Street premises; his share in the bean-business. An accident put paid to his survival rating in that quick and cut-throat world.) In this pleasant garden flat at Hammersmith with its view of the river, the oarsmen on their slender boats, the geese waddling in the blue-grey mud, I turn over my memories. I accuse myself daily from my enforced retirement. I have become an expert analyst of my own errors, a master of pellucid hindsight.

But I could not have legislated for Jimmy. Turn me at the breath of a conjuror's spell into the perfectly responsive lover and he comes on still. Waiting, watching for his opportunity. You played into his hands, Carmen, my love, my loss. You allowed him to take you away from the one person who could have given you something more lasting. That was your choice. Let me not question your right to do so, impair in any way that precious freedom that we boastfully celebrated. That was our undoing.

Carmen was away a great deal in those weeks when Christopher was taking tea with Joanna. Those travel magazines, with their freebies he was too busy to share with her, produced commission after commission. Opportunity after opportunity.

It was around this time that he had to travel out to the

sticks to a factory somewhere beyond Worcester specialising in a hard-wearing, glassy tile whose samples had captivated his current client. He was due to launch himself into the crowded juice-bar market, with three outlets about to open before the end of June, a month behind schedule. Christopher had been unhappy with the first batch of tiles and had been invited down to the factory for a technical session followed by a free lunch, for the manufacturers could see that further orders waited. He fell into conversation on the train to Worcester with a retired railwayman who was travelling on his free pass, changing trains at random, with no particular destination in mind. He was heartbroken at the decline of the great industry in which he had spent his life since 1936 when he had joined the Great Western Railway in Plymouth. Christopher told himself: I am a sucker for these threnodies of the old timers, their on-cue regrets.

The railwayman began with the loss of the men who inspected their lengths of track, loving each tarry sleeper and tailored curve of rail; their replacement by jobsworths who were more interested in admiring the view. He went on to defective signals, criminal under-investment, rudeness, vandalism, locked waiting rooms – and Christopher lapped it up.

"This pass is a good thing [Christopher was dismayed at the sudden appearance of a good thing in this gloomy riff]. If the weather's good, I just say to the wife, let's go off somewhere and off we go. It doesn't matter where."

There was the briefest tremor, like the shadow of a bird's wingbeat over a sunny lawn, which they both recognised. For Christopher had just been told that the wife was dead, three years ago, ten years into the railwayman's retirement. Past and present were getting tangled up. These days, he had only himself to interrogate when the sun brightened the new day. He could no longer make a proposal to 'the wife'. He was alone with his memories: the tapping of wheels with a dull hammer, the whistling of a gang going out along the cutting, a distant chuff of steam.

Carmen, whispers Christopher to himself, is it preposterous to think that we might have grown old together? A pair of wizened pensioners on the up platform, blackbirds carolling in the trees behind the empty station building, a packed lunch, a thermos, a timetable, the sun blazing at its zenith like it does in the classic serials on TV as the merry face of the train appears around the corner. We have spared ourselves that. We have not run the risk of going stale. Yes, that one has been avoided.

When Christopher first became convinced that it was happening, that Jimmy had glided once more into their lives, he blamed himself but then he blamed Carmen and he blamed Jimmy. He was happy to blame anyone who crossed his path because he wanted an explanation. He wanted to know why. He did not want to be told that there was no explanation. He was certainly not ready for that. That would have finished him, he thought, just then. Give me a villain every time. Yield me up a scapegoat and let me get to work.

Jimmy fitted the bill. Christopher supposed that he resented his freedom, his easy assumption of it. His own freedom was the byproduct of a sort of mania. He worked all hours, struggled to keep one step ahead, tore about London in pursuit of fresh commissions. He banked up the money, which eventually overtook what he had accumulated by his inheritance and his lucky investment in the Whitfield Street property. He quite overlooked – in the way that the self-made generally do – that his financial success had its own good measure of luck. This did not, however, prevent him from judging Jimmy. He had never, he reflected sardonically, let hypocrisy stand in his way. Carmen reported to him what she had heard (or had her eyes seen?) of Jimmy's inherited wealth. There was a substantial apartment "on the Riviera" – a studiedly vague form of words which started certain speculations in Christopher's mind – and his apartment near Regent's Park (bought, so she informed him, with the proceeds from the sale of a minor Picasso owned by his banker father). There was the childhood drift through European capitals, a varied but always expensive education, music lessons with the best teachers at every turn, the early debut recital at the Wigmore, the fluke success of the Schoenberg CD (the result of its being used as part of the score for a cult art movie) and the constant, undimmed success with women. Jimmy was not the old style smooth seducer – though the cuckolded and the cheated always represented him as being this. He was the sensitive type, who had learned a few tricks from the feminists, who was never crass. His seductions did not draw on the resources of antique *machismo* but were achieved by subtler means. Women did not feel they were being used or wheedled into bed. He flattered their intelligence; he treated them as equals; he bothered to listen to what they said and to behave as if they were individuals. In return, they loved his modernised *politesse*, that whiff of old money and old manners subtly enjoined with the brash scent of contemporary cool. Even Christopher, when his growling jealous resentment was over, had to admit that it was an admirable act, conceived and executed with perfect timing and timbre.

But then Jimmy was a performer and all the world loves a strolling player, envying a freedom they could have themselves, often enough, if they tried. Am I being somewhat tart, Christopher wondered? Am I letting him get to me? I should think so. I should think it highly likely. He went through various stages of hating Jimmy. The early outrage

– centring first on Carmen herself for her unforgivable betrayal – was succeeded by a focussed loathing for the very notion of Jimmy. Sometimes it was petty and childish. That CD he stamped on, having tossed it to the kitchen floor, picking up the shattered box rather sheepishly, feeling a fool, and feeding it uneasily into the plastic swing-bin. After this he tried to pull himself together. He started to deliver sonorous moral lectures to himself – a tumbler of malt in his hand – about the need, in a contemporary relationship, to avoid the dreary *bourgeois* notion of dutiful monogamy, to adopt an aristocratic notion of sex, of high indifference to where the pleasures of civilised sensuality were sought. But this was equally unsuccessful. For it was not the sexual errancy that hurt him most, it was the loss of intimacy, the loss of that intense bond which he thought they both enjoyed, Carmen and he, but which was now ruptured. For good? Even at that stage (which he later discovered to be the second of her three fatal loops of dalliance with Jimmy) he hoped that she would tire, that she would return to him, that the ineffable seducer would move on to newer, sweeter, grass at the top of the meadow.

She did return, by which time he was fatally compromised with Joanna. Christopher now moved quickly to terminate that little episode. He had exhausted the possibilities of his English rose who in turn was now consumed with guilt and resolved to return to Carl, to make him her new project of improvement. "I think we need to work on our relationship" she informed Christopher solemnly at their last *al fresco* lunch. All this talk of work, rendering love down to a task, he found sharply anaphrodisiac. He was glad to be discharged.

~ TWO ~

Carl had rather not have found out. In view of subsequent events, he was very clear about that.

Joanna insisted on dragging him to a distant friend of a friend, who had set up as a therapist. She said they must work on their relationship. Carl did not like such talk which seemed to him, anyway, to carry within it the seeds of its own failure. If we must work on our marriage then surely it is doomed. He was sorry. He was a practical man. He did not work with approximations. He liked exactness.

The consulting-room (Carl considered that this was probably not the correct term) was on the ground floor of a substantial terraced house in North London. One ascended a short flight of steps and opened a heavy door which, he couldn't help noticing from the drag across the tiles, marked by a scoured arc, needed some easement. He believed that he would have offered there and then to remedy the situation had he been carrying his tools. They stepped across the threshold, Joanna leading the way with her usual dogged badge of courage, then passed in to the front room through a door on the left. It was furnished very simply. Not exactly the bleakness of a waiting room or surgery, but a little frigid, Carl thought. There was a beige fitted carpet, four or five armchairs arranged in a companionable circle, a dull print of (if he was not mistaken) Monet's lilies covering most of the end wall, a small console on which were a TV set and video recorder and a stereo sound system, and a low circular table at the epicentre of the arrangement of chairs. A single, white ceramic vase of yellow roses stood on the wide window sill. The Venetian blinds were three-quarters open. Everything was neat and tidy. It did not have the feel of a room that was ever used for the ordinary, messy business of living. The therapist, who lost no time in instructing them to address her as Helen, left the room to make some tea. They said nothing to each other but looked around. They were uncomfortable and apprehensive. When Helen returned with the tea she smiled at them as if they were imbeciles or perhaps small children being offered a treat. Carl thought she noticed his hostility but it seemed to fire her up with enthusiasm. She threw herself into the business with vigour.

"Now, Carl and Joanna, I am so pleased that you wanted to come today. I want you to think of this morning as a sort of introduction, a getting-to-know-you session. I think the fact that you are both here is a sign that already you are wanting to work through to a solution. This is what we all want and I am confident that everything can be resolved, that we can work together towards a new start. Tea?"

As her patter came out, Carl's apprehensions began to leave their lurking places. He regretted having come but he knew that this was just what Helen wanted. It would confirm her knowledge of human behaviour, reward her redemptive skills. She would enjoy disarming him, curing him of his predictable resistances. She had seen it all before. All it needed was some work. But did he want to work on his relationship? How had it come to this?

Carl knew that in Joanna's circle of friends he was considered to lack sophistication. He was seen to work with his hands, to be interested in cars, to have little time for cultural activities. Perhaps Joanna thought that he had married her on false pretences. Their meeting was quite by chance. He had finished his professional studies and had decided to visit Paris for a few weeks, looking after a flat that belonged to one of his father's business associates. In those days he painted. Not very well, but it amused him. One morning he set up his little easel on one of the *quais* and started to paint one of those scenes which appear on all the postcards. He supposed now that, had he possessed more originality, he would have chosen some other subject but he had found a suitable perch across the road on the steps of a building which seemed shut and which gave him a good perspective on the bookstands and the river flowing behind them, with taller buildings in the background on the right bank. It was a hot day and, from time to time, people would come and sit at the other end of the long stone step to rest or to consult their gazeteer or drink some refreshment. They also tried to see what he was doing and generally they smiled. The public always feels well-disposed to an artist at work, however indifferent it will become later.

He had nearly finished his humdrum scene when he became aware of a pretty young woman to his left at the far end of the step. She was delicately licking an ice-cream. She returned his smile and, rather nervously, got up and came over to see what he was doing. There was something schoolgirlish about her but he judged she must have been nineteen or twenty. She said she liked the painting and then, rather abruptly, she asked if it would be for sale. Carl laughed. The notion had never occurred to him. His few previous attempts had been given away to relatives. With an improvisatory boldness that still astonished him in retrospect he announced that if she would have a coffee with him when he had finished, she could have it for nothing. She burst out into giggles while he blinked at his own *chutzpah*. They had coffee, in the course of which they discovered that we were both alone in Paris, for largely the same reasons, and therefore it was a natural progress – notwithstanding their mutual shyness and awkwardness – to discuss the matter of an evening meal.

And now, in this carpeted room, Carl looked across at Joanna. She had not changed in outward appearance. Perhaps he too looked the same. He could not believe that either of them had changed inwardly to any great degree. So what had brought them to this brink of absurdity? Why were they putting their lives in the hands of this smiling woman who treated them, as we treat the old, as if they were tiny children who cannot help themselves. He got to his feet, shaking with anger and frustration. The therapist was used to this sort of reaction. Without getting up she put out her hand and pulled down firmly on Carl's forearm. Dully, he complied with the gesture and sank back into his chair. But he was not listening to the unfolding patter, its rhythms of reassurance.

There was indeed a gulf between them. He was the gauche student dabbling crudely in oils and she was the shy young woman whose parents lived in a red-roofed house overlooking a long garden which ran down to a railway line that took you to Waterloo station in twenty-seven minutes. Carl made a first, halting visit to the house one summer Saturday. There were striped canvas club chairs set out in a large semicircle – not unlike this arrangement of armchairs in North London. There was a rug on the lawn and Joanna, giggling, led him down to where her parents were sitting waiting to inspect him. Her father was all red-faced bluster and the mother anxiously polite. Carl felt their eyes on him. He felt the work of assessment being started. He did not then know that it would never end, that they would not cease to judge him, to find him wanting. And eventually Joanna herself would succumb. She, too, would compute his failings, draw up the end-of-year accounts. Were they right to suspect him? In view of how things turned out, he reflected, were their fears not all too well-founded?

On that summer afternoon he tried not to put a foot

wrong. Joanna helped by squeezing his arm, whispering encouragement, letting him know that the verdict was: so far so good. Tea was brought. A heavy cake. A cat came down the lawn to add its professional weight to the process of assessing and inspecting. He could hear the voices of neighbours, the whooping cries of children in an inflatable paddling-pool on the other side of the fence, the periodic rattle of a Southern Region train at the foot of the garden. Joanna's father was a solicitor coasting down the last short slope to retirement. His wife was much younger than he and valiant in good works. Once or twice Carl felt an urge to howl like some imprisoned beast but for the most part he did what was expected of him. He thought it had gone well until, when he eventually reached the moment when it was decent to propose that he go, Joanna's father came over to him and put his hand on his shoulder and said: "Very nice to have met you Carl. You must come again." What was odd was the intonation, the faint air of menace as if he were threatening him, defying him to have the brass gall ever to come near his daughter again. Carl could not decide what he had done wrong. Like any young man of twenty he was encumbered with a sense of general inadequacy but he could not identify any particular misdemeanour. Joanna dismissed his reservations – rather unconvincingly, he thought – and claimed that it had all gone well. "They liked you," she said, in a rather brisk, matter-of-fact tone.

Not long after this they went to a party on the other side of London. They stayed over by arrangement and, to their mutual surprise, had their first sexual experience. Joanna henceforth behaved like someone who has suddenly, and rather unexpectedly, discovered a new hobby. She was always perfectly decorous and outwardly ever the well-brought up Surrey girl but her sexual appetite turned out to be remarkably vigorous. Carl had to struggle to keep up with her inventive energy. They kept in touch during the year of their first jobs (she was doing a diploma in librarianship at one end of the country, he was adding a diploma in interior design to his professional portfolio at the other) and they had as many weekends together as they could manage. Carl met her parents again but on these occasions they seemed to have withdrawn into their shell. He could not get much from them beyond pleasantries and even that hostile gleam in her father's eye seemed to have dulled. As Carl and Joanna drifted towards marriage the parents merely acquiesced in what now seemed inevitable. Two weeks before the wedding, the old man (as he had come to seem) was hurled by a sudden coronary forwards on to his roaring petrol mower which dragged him several yards down the slope to the hydrangeas. His wife reacted to his death by appearing to shrink before their eyes in the subsequent months. She did not long survive him and with the proceeds of that cream-coloured 1930s villa they bought a large flat in central London and had a series of expensive trips around the world. Joanna almost wilfully buried the skills in garden and home that her mother had dinned into her but Carl suspected that they were merely dormant and would start to show themselves again before very long.

By now he was successful and very busy indeed. Joanna was made redundant from her college library after a re-organisation and showed no desire to find an alternative post. She dabbled in the history of art and developed a collecting interest in early twentieth century craft furniture. It was about this time – long before Carl had any evidence of her involvement with Christopher – that he began to suspect that she may have been (in ways and through opportunities he could not quite imagine) gratifying her other passions. Perhaps, Carl considered, they should have found their way to the therapists earlier than they did. But this was a story of too little done too late, an inventory of errors. Which makes it the usual story.

The therapist, preliminaries over, had barely launched herself on to the main menu, when Carl stood up, this time in no mood to be fobbed off. She smiled tolerantly. She was professionally incapable of being taken by surprise. She would weave him back into the sublime circle of her special spell. When it became apparent that he was determined to resist her, the mood changed. She darkened. She looked on him with contempt and even her sisterly solicitation towards Joanna ebbed – as if she too were part of the conspiracy against her. No longer was it a matter of their throwing away their chance to rescue themselves from the wind-lashed rock of dysfunction. The couple were showing their contempt for the therapist's very metaphysic: her look contained no hint of possible forgiveness. Carl led the way and Joanna (who might have been expected to have put up a fight) meekly followed. Civilised abuse followed them down the hall (later there would be softened pleadings, wheedlings) and they passed out into the blur of noise and traffic and low-level drabness that was Kentish Town Road.

Joanna walked behind Carl, sullen and wordless. He too said nothing. He flagged down a cab and they got in without any histrionic 'scene' of the kind married couples so frequently cleave to. The cab-driver ostentatiously adjusted his mirror in order to inspect his fare. Evidently, he judged it prudent to leave them to simmer in silence. They were spared his jaunty observations and nuggets of folk wisdom. Back at the flat they collapsed on the long sofa and Carl went out to fetch a bottle of wine and two glasses. Joanna laughed when she saw this and her mood improved rapidly. He realised that she too had dreaded the encounter from which they had just forcibly rescued themselves. Because of her apparent enthusiasm in making the arrangements Carl had wrongly jumped to the conclusion that it was a process she wanted to go through with. It was the spirit of her mother in her: the need to be seen to be doing the right thing, even if it was the wrong thing. Setting one's face against inertia. They held each other. They kissed. They became more intimate still. Thus they ended the day on a note of rising expectation that, out of this knot of tangled paths, the way would become clear. If it did not, Carl reflected, then the blame was his. He need not have done what he did. He need not have put at risk this fragile hope of a resolution.

Carl found out by accident. There is, of course, no other way to make the necessary discovery. Three disparate pieces of data came together. One of his men casually mentioned that he had seen Joanna lunching nearby. This in itself was not implausible or problematic. She frequently lunched with girlfriends – or, in truth, with friends of any gender – since her husband was so rarely available. For some reason Carl asked about her companion – evidently with too little finesse to prevent the lifting of a head, the exchange of a glance amongst the workforce. He thought he detected a certain reluctance to share speculations with him. Generally oblivious to the details of her daily routine which Joanna ran past him at breakfast, this time he remembered that she had said she was out on a field trip to the Ashmolean that day. And, finally, they had tickets for a show which – again so rare were these excursions – was always followed by a meal out, an indulgence for which she always prepared by rigid abstinence from any mid-day meal. Even poor dull Carl could see the ignition of a spark from the conjunction of all these elements.

Gloomily, like a character in the shabby melodrama this was becoming, he made an excuse and left the shop with its whining drills, stacked planks, and curled shavings on the sawdusted floor. He knew the restaurant, which had helpfully been identified, and knew that it was opposite a coffee bar with another entrance in a side street through which he could dip unseen. He settled with a paper cup of coffee amongst the listless office-workers and set up his tawdry observation post. The restaurant was able to drop the upper part of its street-facing window which gave diners the advantage of *al fresco* dining without the disadvantages of being importuned by flower-sellers, beggars, hawkers and miscellaneous madmen of the street. Above the row of colourful window boxes he caught sight of Joanna. She was sitting across a table from Christopher, whom Carl knew as the restaurant-fitter who had come to his aid several weeks previously. They were intent on conversation but he could not say, even in his feverish condition, that they displayed any especial intimacy, any fuel for his outrage. Joanna looked out of sorts and Christopher seemed to be pleading with her. Neither looked in the least bit comfortable. At one point he tried to put his hand on her arm as a calming gesture but she withdrew it sharply. So far, so good, thought the amateur gumshoe. Then, as if she regretted this stab of coldness, she leaned forward and placed her hand around the back of Christopher's neck. They looked at each other in this next frame of Carl's silent movie for several seconds.

Then she pulled him to her and kissed him more than briefly. Carl leapt to his feet, blundered out of the coffee-bar leaving a trail of upset cartons and trays in his wake. He strode across the street and stood below the box of bright blooms, bellowing some coarse and almost certainly uninventive obscenity. Joanna, alarmed, got to her feet. Christopher remained seated. He seemed curiously relaxed, as if he had no reason to show any discomfort or unease at the intruder's ruffian-like arrival. This had the effect of maddening Carl still further. He stepped on to the narrow strip of tiles in order to bring himself closer to their trysting-place and lunged at Christopher. The latter ducked neatly then stood up, retreating into the interior of the restaurant. Carl was off balance and, steadying himself, reached out for something to hold on to. His mistake was to grasp one of the window plant troughs which were unsecured. The whole thing came away from the hinged wooden shelf beneath the window and landed on the pavement. Passers-by were now expressing interest. A small crowd had gathered and a beefy type decided to act as referee. Carl planted on him the blow he had prepared for Christopher. Outraged, the man swung back at Carl and (he discovered later when he came round with a sore head in a small confined space which he discovered in horror to be a police cell) laid him out.

Later, Carl found out that the police had been called. Naturally the version of events least favourable to himself was given out as the first draft of this miserable history. He was dragged off. Joanna followed and, with great effort, succeeded in minimising the consequences, heading off charges, calming the whole affair. Carl was soon sent packing and returned to the flat, where Joanna chose to say as little as possible, the urge to reproach him battling against the perceived discomfort of her own position. He sank, in the ensuing days, into a deep depression. He hated himself for this exhibition of brawling barbarism, for allowing himself to traduce his better nature, for his lack of self-control. And Carl hated what he had seen, hated the knowledge, hated the image of Joanna at that open window, framed by flowers, reaching out to that smooth little bastard in the denim shirt.

Carmen's official bulletin to Christopher specified a travel trade conference in Italy. She did indeed fly there late one Thursday night but, mercifully, she was not required to ply her trade. She found these shindigs unspeakable, a grievous affront to the soul of those who were not directly engaged with their arcane purposes. Her early journalistic success had ensured that her experience of these events was much less extensive than that of her colleagues, many of whom had cut their professional teeth on them. But she had seen quite enough. The clouds of cant that buzzed like a fine mist of evening insects around the heads of the delegates, proudly trussed and labelled, guffawing and – oh, the language hurt her still! – 'networking', made her grit her teeth. Clutching the bland press hand-outs which obviated the need to sit in the halls listening to the numbing 'presentations' of industry leaders, annotating the jokes carefully inserted in the script at the expense of the colourless characters currently enjoying favour as President or Chairman of whatever Association was sponsoring the event, Carmen would circle around little groups, pressing herself on them, unconvincingly lending an ear to their special pleading and institutionalised whines in the vain hope of gathering a 'story', but longing in truth to be released.

Yes, she flew to Italy to join Jimmy. He had been taking part in a contemporary music festival in one of the Tuscan cities and had booked, as his reward, an apartment in a small villa at what turned out to be a very busy seaside resort south of Viareggio. The beach was wide and flat and the couple would begin each day with a swim taken before the beach became impossibly peopled. The villa was altogether more tranquil. It had been skilfully partitioned to yield the maximum amount of privacy for each apartment. Although Carmen and Jimmy did not have a direct sea view, their bedroom window looked out onto a grove of olive trees and one of lemons. A small doorway to which they alone enjoyed access opened on to the groves and, from this secluded area, they could also slip in and out of an iron gate that gave on to a small avenue, back from the sea, flanked by cropped mulberry trees.

This was a happy interlude – Carmen later concluded from her inability to remember much about it. For five days they swam, ate, talked, laughed, loved and felt free. They talked a great deal about freedom. That she did remember.

"Why don't I feel freer than I do?" Carmen asked Jimmy one evening as they swung in a canopied canvas seat set against the wall of the villa. The last rays of sun were filtering through the leaves of the lemon trees and they were drinking a cool, dry wine, their glasses on an iron table set in front of them.

"Well, you're not making too bad a job of it."

"But this feels like an interlude, a parenthesis. It isn't going to last is it?"

"Why do you say that? Just enjoy it."

"But that's my point. It isn't easy."

"It isn't easy because you have made a fetish of your precious work. You don't know how to relax, to appreciate ease. It's an art like any other."

"Meaning?"

"Like any art you have to balance a talent for it, and a feel for it, with the discipline to work at it, to discover its special signature. Just as you can't sit down at a piano and deliver a finished Chopin sonata without practice, study, thought, so you can't achieve creative indolence in an instant, especially given the mania of *your* working life."

Carmen nestled against Jimmy, sipped her glass, plucking a fragment of seed that had landed on its surface and dropping it to the ground.

"I like the sound of that creative indolence, but you think it's beyond me?"

"I think it's beyond most people now. The means that have given them the potential for leisure are the same that prevent them realising it: all that restless energy, change, discontent, 'dynamism'."

"This isn't, is it, going to be a seminar on the Protestant Work Ethic?"

"Not if you don't want it to be. But that has a lot to answer for. I don't see why one shouldn't ask, from time to time, what piling up all that hard-earned cash is actually for. I'm not arguing for idleness. That would be stultifying. I'm saying that some things aren't the product of furious attack. And they may turn out to be the most important things. The things that make us most fully alive."

"Are you going to become a missionary? I can imagine you somewhere like this, running courses for the stinking rich in how to take it easy. Self-improvement is where the dosh is today and what could be more attractive to the people with money to throw away than learning – not how to lose weight or shed an addiction, which are painful – but how to be indolent? What's that Italian phrase?"

"*Dolce far niente.*"

"How about it?"

"It sounds like too much hard work. More wine?"

"Please. But seriously, I think I know what you are saying. When I look at the life Christopher and I have been living in London I can't say it *satisfies* us. I think most of our friends are in the same predicament."

"You should travel. It's the answer to most things. I

move about a lot in my work, naturally, but I mean real travel, letting oneself drift, letting oneself be caught in unexpected places, staying on. Then moving on. Knowing when it's right to do so. Taking the world's pulse."

"I mean to, one day."

"Don't delay it for too long."

"I'll try."

Jimmy shifted in the swing-seat, took a long draught of wine. Carmen could see that he wanted to say something that was going to be difficult for him.

"Do you mind if I talk about Christopher?"

"If you want to. What is there to say?"

"Oh I don't mean one of those conversations 'about us'. This is hard to say, but I don't want you to throw something away that means more to you than perhaps you realise."

"What? Is this a subtle warning about Jimmy the philanderer? Don't get too comfortable because you may be about to be ditched?"

"Don't be absurd. I think we both know where things stand. I don't think either of us has any illusions."

"Jimmy, you are an incurable romantic. Just what a girl wants to hear in a Tuscan lemon grove at night."

"You know exactly what I mean. What are you going to do on Sunday night?"

"OK. I'm flying back. But why do we have to compute this? It's like what you were just saying about travel. Let's just enjoy it. See what happens."

"You said you thought he might be seeing someone."

"Oh, I don't know. I can hardly get on my high horse. I don't suppose it's anything serious. Or perhaps it is. Look, Jimmy, it's too late for me to act out the perfect marriage playlet. Not with my track record. Some things can't be retrieved. Replayed. I've made mistakes. I haven't always got it right. Correction. I've seldom got it right. That happens to be the way it is. I'm not the sort of person who wants to work at a relationship."

"Sounds like the activity of a coal miner at the seam."

"Precisely. Let's have a little of the *dolce far niente*. Let's have a little natural spontaneity. If Christopher and I ever get back together it will happen. I can't make it happen."

"I don't want you to go back to him, naturally."

"Not today, at any rate."

"Am I that much of a rake?"

"He called you a 'sexual opportunist' which I thought was quite good for him."

"And what do you think?"

"I've no idea. I'm tired of judging people, pigeon-holing them, giving them labels."

"I thought that was what you did for a living and called it style journalism."

"Yes, yes. In fact it is precisely because I do it for a living that it has started to disgust me."

"Which brings us back to where we started. Freedom."

"Right. I am a convert. Can we have lesson one of your exacting course in how to be free?"

Jimmy laughed. He pointed to the winking lights of a jet travelling across the night sky towards Pisa or Rome. It was getting cooler. They huddled against each other for warmth. The scent in the garden was rich and sweet. The air that bore it was cool and clear. Occasionally a shout came from the direction of the beach. A car went past along the little avenue. This seemed like freedom enough. Somewhere beneath it all, like a buried watercourse, flowed all sorts of knotted problems, dilemmas. Responsibilities, if you will. But tonight Carmen felt utterly relaxed with Jimmy. Utterly relaxed with night in this place and at this time.

Their Tuscan interlude ended all too quickly. Jimmy had

to fly on to Vienna. Carmen had to return to London which, at Heathrow, was grey and cold and wet – though it was officially summer. A knot of drunken louts had spoiled the flight with their vicious language and uncontrolled behaviour. Somewhere over the Alps, Carmen turned round and gave them a look of disapproval. One of the young men staggered to his feet, unsteady from drink. His belly heaved in a dirty white T-shirt which bore – oddly she thought – a £ sign. He breathed his tinned beer over her as he brought his face close to hers.

"Have you got a problem darling?"

She tried to ignore him. Experience had taught her that the last thing one should do was allow oneself to become engaged in a dialogue from which it would prove impossible to extricate oneself.

"Can't speak can ya? Lost your fuckin' tongue?"

His eyes swam mistily. He had difficulty remaining upright. She noticed that on the upper part of his four fingers, above the knuckle, the letters L-O-V-E were tattooed in pale blue.

"You're not a fucking Eytie are you? Speaka da English darling? You know what you need love. My fuckin' prescription. A good shag."

His fellows whooped with delighted laughter. "Give her one, Garry."

"I might just do that. I might just do that."

As he swayed uncertainly an air-steward came down the aisle and expertly lifted the man under the arms, guiding him carefully back to his seat into which he slumped gratefully. The other passengers seemed relieved. They looked across at Carmen, sending that expressive signal of weary acceptance that she knew so well from previous incidents of this kind. There was a look of quiet distaste on the face of a working class couple in their late sixties who occupied the seats across from hers. They appeared hurt and baffled, as if they could not understand where such behaviour came from, why it seemed to have established itself as a norm that all of them seemed powerless to oppose.

Carmen passed out of the airport into the Underground and was home inside an hour. She sensed immediately that Christopher was uneasy, that something had happened. She waited to find out what it was that she was to be told. He came through to the living room with a cafetière of fresh coffee which he placed on that long ash table he had made himself. He lay back against the soft leather of the sofa.

"You missed all the fun. Carl went a little over the top today."

"Carl? I thought he was the most phlegmatic man in London. I'd like to have been around to see him losing his cool."

"I was having lunch with Joanna."

Christopher's boldness, his frank, unapologetic tone did not ring entirely true. It felt like a calculated strategy, like someone trying to clear the ground for the launch of trickier matter. Entering into the spirit of the thing, she decided to play the spiteful bitch.

"That must have been nice for the two of you. Was she as radiant as ever, little Jo?"

Her own moral position was so doubtful after five days with Jimmy that she wasn't planning to overdo this line of approach.

"She was fine. We bumped into each other in Berwick Street and I suggested lunch. We went to La Barca."

"You must take me there some time."

Christopher looked at her with distaste, as if she were deliberately trying to lower the tone of their encounter.

"We were just quietly eating when Carl bounded up

from nowhere and took a swing at me. There was a sort of tussle and someone came out of the crowd to break us up and copped a blow meant for me. It was a bit farcical in fact. The guy then hit back at Carl and laid him out. The police arrived and took him away. Joanna was distraught."

"Poor dear."

"Is that all you can offer: cheap sarcasms?"

"Well, I can do lethally honed satire if you prefer."

"Did you enjoy your holiday in the sun?"

"No holiday. Being surrounded by a lot of travel industry types. It would put you off going on holiday for life."

"There's no need to keep up the pretence, Car, I've spoken to Marianne. There was no conference in Viareggio. I know about Jimmy, too, so can we cut the crap?"

"Fine, so let's get straight to the interesting bits. What was Carl doing brawling in Berwick Street? Did he have some reason for getting overexcited at his wife's pleasantly unexpected lunch with an old friend? And, please, don't offer me any of the usual explanations."

"I don't think either of us is in a position to squat on the moral high ground."

"So you have been fucking her."

"Do you have to be so crude?"

"Oh, it's to be expected. I'm a rough Northern girl. We call a spade a ruddy shovel where I come from. Do you think I'm incapable of noticing anything? Do you think I was dreamily lapping up the taciturn charm of dopey Carl while you two were cosying up that night in the restaurant? Give me some credit for having eyes in my head."

Christopher poured out the coffee. He stared into the surface of his mug. He rubbed his eyes and suddenly looked terribly tired. For the first time since she had returned Carmen felt sorry for him. She felt sorry for herself, too. What had become of them? How had they got into this predicament? She did not want to talk about Jimmy. She could not entirely understand a rather strange reaction she always had after spending some time with him. Intense and vivid as her encounters with him were – for Jimmy was always a wonderfully animating presence and Italy had been a special period of grace – once he had gone the atmosphere quickly faded. She could hardly now recall what they had done together, what they had talked about, what had kept them both so enraptured. For she was convinced, in retrospect, that they had been enraptured. It was like a dream whose vividness barely survives the moment of waking. But was she, hard-bitten Carmen, the victim of a sort of schoolgirl fantasy? Was she, perhaps, merely Jimmy's plaything? One of his many playthings? She found herself thinking of Alice and the presence of both of them in Paris not so long ago. Their apparent prior awareness that they were both to be there. Carmen was not the sort of person who liked to be duped. She liked to think she was in control but, suddenly, she felt helpless. She reached out to Christopher but he refused to respond. She felt his arm stiff and unwelcoming. She supposed each of them was silently taking the measure of the other's legitimate outrage. Surely he could see this? Surely he could see that she needed him? That they needed each other?

After several minutes silence, with each of them prostrate on the sofa, sullen and intransigent, she raised herself and poured out some coffee. She wanted to be refreshed. She wanted to find a way out of this silliness. She wanted them to beat a path back to the crossroads where they had taken the wrong turning, but could it now be identified? Swinging through the automatic doors at the airport she had felt so alive and certain and purposeful. She had been riding high. Yet now she seemed to have collapsed inwardly. More than this, she seemed to feel a sort of quiet terror stealing over her. She could no longer discern any bearings. In a matter of seconds her world had collapsed and she had an unpleasant sensation that she was the architect of her own misfortune, that even Christopher was a victim of her delinquency. Had she driven him to this absurd dalliance with the negligible Joanna? Was everything, simply, her fault?

She wrapped her hands around the coffee mug and rocked herself slowly backwards and forwards on the edge of the sofa. She did not dare bring her eyes round and look Christopher in the face. She did not dare risk the request for forgiveness being refused.

Carmen's return from Italy was marked by a brief show-down with Christopher which ended in an unsatisfactory silence, a brooding, ambiguous peace which lasted for several days. Both were trying to find a way to get to the bottom of what had happened. Events had overtaken them, demolishing their usual libertarian conviction that nothing really mattered but the pursuit of intelligent pleasure, the connoisseurship of experience, doing as one pleased with no more than a loose do-as-one-would-be-done-by ethic to mark off its indistinct limits. Something had changed, yet quite what that change had been and what its implications were for both of them remained to be calibrated. In the case of Christopher, to be witness to that short blow which felled Carl in a London street – absurd slapstick that it was, from one point of view – had proved the catalyst. To this point he had not lived his life in this way – with the coarse plotline of a soap opera. He expected things to proceed more gently, without such stark confrontations. Plainly, from now on, they would not abide by this rule.

He saw Carl some time after this. He expected a difficult encounter but Carl was oddly conciliatory. Christopher's brief relationship with Joanna was over. He had neither seen nor spoken to her since she ran from the restaurant that day (where, as Carl no doubt now knew, they had been scattering their fistfuls of earth on its corpse). Perhaps, in some perverse sort of way, Carl was grateful to him for restoring them to each other, for inject-ing something into the bloodstream of their relationship. The two men were working in the same street again, a quieter one shaded by plane trees between Tottenham Court Road and Gower Street. They were having coffee at a café with a little terrace overlooking a quaint art deco filling station that must have been there since the 1920s. Carl held out his hand as they sat down.

"No hard feelings."

There was something slightly comical about this, as if he were offering consolation after having beaten one at a game of squash. But he was not being facetious or sly. That was not Carl's way. He was always deadly serious. Christopher mumbled something to indicate that he accepted his goodwill and wished the matter to be at an end. He added quickly that Joanna had gone down to Surrey to supervise the transfer of an elderly relative into a nursing home.

"I think it's the best thing all round, especially now that Joanna is starting a new job."

"A new job?"

Christopher didn't want to spoil things by showing too keen an interest. In fact he did not wish Joanna to be a subject at all.

"Yes, she's doing a temporary job at the Senate House Library."

He jerked his thumb in the direction of the grey bunkers on the far side of Gower Street.

"Her relative isn't really capable any more of looking after herself so it seems the best thing."

It is always the best thing.

"I'm not sure her family ever took to me you know. Especially her father."

Christopher looked across at Carl. He was not the sort of man who confides much in other men. He almost never spoke about personal matters. Christopher wasn't even sure whether he had any real friends or intimates. This contributed, he thought, to a certain air of sadness that lingered about him. He was a perfectly decent man who did not know how to give anything of himself to others. Had he been able to do so he might have had a much happier life. Christopher supposed that brought out certain instincts in Joanna. She would rescue him, make him her project. And now she had an extra reason to take him in hand, to atone for her wickedness. The library job was clearly part of the new order of things.

"I think her father decided, almost from the start, that I didn't measure up in some fashion. They only had the one child and I fancy that he wanted a boy who might be trained up to take over the firm – one of those fusty high street family solicitors who do everything (eventually). Since there was only Joanna, a husband might be the next best thing. I was not a lawyer. An architect wasn't the same thing at all. Her mother also seemed to be uncertain about me. Joanna never wanted to talk about that. She had her own problems and didn't want to mix mine up with them. I gave up trying to understand families years ago. I some-times wish – vindictively no doubt – that he could have had a son just so that he could watch him grow up to refuse to do what he wanted – by opening a gay bar or joining the army – just to teach him that one can't always plan other people's lives for them. I've never grasped this obsession with handing on the baton, perpetuating the family name, keeping the show on the road."

"Perhaps that's because we're in such an ephemeral business. This place I'm doing up as a sushi restaurant used to sell computer supplies. In three years' time it could be a travel agent. And how long is Souper Kitchen going to last?"

"Until my early retirement, I hope."

Carl laughed, and as the two men sat there on the terrace in the sun Christopher felt uncomfortable about the wrong he had done him – though Carl seemed to be thriving on it. It was he who was floundering, not sure which direction to take.

"Do you know, we went to a therapist," he suddenly said, adopting a deliberately brisk and matter of fact tone.

"I didn't. Was it helpful?"

"I didn't allow it to be. I am afraid I walked out. I thought Joanna would be furious with me but she later admitted that she was grateful to me for pulling the plug. I think you have to be the right sort of people for therapy."

"What sort is that?"

"Well, it's partly tolerating the lingo. But I suppose I mean you have to believe in advance that it's going to work. You have to begin with faith. And then there's a sort of underlying thing I can't get along with which Joanna – quite cleverly I thought – called The Utopian Premiss. The notion that all problems can be solved provided you apply yourself. Provided you put yourself in the hands of the professional. I suppose neither of us really believed that. Which made things rather hard for the therapist. She was a professional. She believed she could solve the problem. So our walking out was a kind of insult. And you know how solemn and self-righteous these people are. It all got very nasty."

"Are you going to tell me that you sorted things out by yourselves?"

"Something like that. I mean to say, we're not living in Utopia but we've come to see that we both took a wrong road, that we needed to retrace our steps. It's not the same as before. It's as if we were now walking carefully round an unexploded mine. It makes you more careful. More thoughtful. More appreciative of the importance of getting things right. Does that make any sense?"

"A lot. I think Joanna is worth getting right."

Carl looked at Christopher quickly and shrewdly.

Perhaps, thought Christopher, he was looking to see if he were saying more than his words allowed, as if there were a part of her he had still not surrendered. He need not have worried. Christopher was glad that they had retrieved their not-quite-Utopia. He was unhappy with his role because he felt that he had trifled with Joanna. Perhaps even exploited her – though she was an adult and far less naïve than she made herself seem. This visible putting right of things reassured him that he had not done lasting damage. For a wry moment he even wondered if he had actually done some lasting good.

Carl then said that he must go. His work awaited him. Christopher said he would sit for a little longer to finish his coffee though he knew that he too should not have been wasting time. Left to himself he watched a large, expensive car slide into the little filling station from a side street. A man in a neat suit and a russet brown hat got out, rather overdressed for a summer's day, Christopher thought. The man was a well-preserved seventy-five, and Christopher surmised that he was a successful and rich businessman. He moved with a rather dignified formality and his manner in addressing the pump attendant seemed that of someone who was accustomed, across a lifetime, to deference, to quiet daily recognition on the part of those beneath him in the social hierarchy, that they were below and he was above them and that was that. It was not an arrogant swagger, more a simple acceptance of the obvious fact that he was of another type. This started a reflection, as Christopher drained the last of his coffee, that he was working for a different class, the capital's proliferating *nouveaux riches*. These were people who did not wear their privileges lightly. Rather they flaunted them constantly like someone waving a flag of semaphore. They took careful note of which fashions to copy, they had an encylopaedic knowledge of brand

names and of what was the most expensive, the most osten-
tatious, the most noticeable thing. And Christopher was
one of them for he worked to anticipate their tastes. They
were the people he was servicing, their values were his
values, yet he could not help himself, from time to time,
finding something comic in the solemnity of their materialism, their conviction of the importance of money and of the
simple – almost childish – connections they perceived
between its power and what it would confer on them. Their
talk of it in truth betrayed their uncertainty, their insecurity,
their lack of that simple social confidence he had seen on
the face of the kempt septuagenarian with his upright walk
and kid driving gloves and gleaming brogues.

That night Christopher walked back to Whitfield Street
in a more reflective mood than was customary with him. It
was still light at nine o'clock. The outdoor restaurant tables
in Charlotte Street were busy. The atmosphere was gratifyingly festive. On an impulse he sat down at the
lemon-coloured table of a Greek restaurant and dialled
Carmen on his mobile. She responded eagerly to his suggestion of eating out and was at his table by the time the waiter
had brought out the wine he had ordered in anticipation of
her arrival. Her manner recently had been unusually solicitous and so, he supposed, had his own. They had both
wandered and had both returned to each other, feeling their
way back, doing so with gestures that were sometimes exaggerated, sometimes uncomfortable, always charged with a
sense that they should perhaps be more careful in future of
their life together, not treating it with such insouciance. Was
this a sign of incipient middle age?

Carmen draped a black sweater over her bare shoulders
(July in London was warm but not *that* warm) and their
glasses clinked. Quickly, the plates of *meze* began to arrive
and they began to talk. He told her about his conversation

earlier in the day with Carl. When he mentioned Joanna's name she merely smiled. Brawling dissection of their mutal infidelities – the pastime of recent nights – had now given way to tactful forgetting. Christopher could not even be sure that a decent argument would ensue. This studied sweetness did not come naturally to them but they persevered. The open air and late-sinking sunshine helped to create a sympathetic backdrop. He sensed that Carmen wanted to talk but in ways that were not usual for her. He tried to make it easier with certain facetious clearances and smoothing-downs.

Carmen also tried, Christopher believed. He never loved her so much as he did during that fragmentary time – during that warm, easy summer. He felt that she had come back to him, willingly, so that they could live again as they had lived before, so that they could recoup their triumphs. He was deceived. The spectre of Jimmy had not been expunged from their *al fresco* feast. He genuinely believed, however, as he recalled that night, that she had convinced herself that she had let him go, that she did not wish to return to him. That she did return was a calamity. But it was an eventuality that seemed quite remote, if not impossible, as they resumed their voyaging from that twilit terrace. Today, as he presses his face against this long window, looking down on the river at low tide, at the detritus on its exposed banks, at the antics of the wading birds, he tastes again the special flavour of that moment which he did not know to be an interlude merely, a graceful exception, but which seemed to him like the restoration of joy, a gift of permanence. For his foolishness, for his refusal to learn the lessons of experience he repents – if there is anyone out there who is willing to listen to his confession.

Carmen talked to him about Jimmy the public figure, carefully removing from her narrative any personal details, any fragments of intimacy, as if she were trying to say that this was the new Jimmy she had constructed for both of them: the friend with an international profile, the serious musician, the name. Christopher was glad to play along with this game. He could see that, if they were to convince themselves of its truth, then it might work. Slowly, he introduced the topic of Joanna – whose retirement from the scene was much more definite now that she and Carl had renewed their life together. These last details, fresh from today's narrative of the wounded husband, were listened to by Carmen with eager attentiveness. Perhaps too eager. Notwithstanding his total absorption in this process of reconciliation and cordial forgetting he could not help noticing – or perhaps he merely imagined that he noticed – a certain light of triumph (shaded, fitful) in Carmen's eye as he confirmed the facts of Joanna's extinction as a living subject in their little pageant. Momentarily, he had an intuition of the inequalities, so to speak, in the balance of power. He could not be certain that Jimmy would vanish with the same alacrity as Joanna.

"When is his next concert?" Christopher inquired pleasantly.

"I'm not sure. But he's bound to post us a flyer. I think there was to be a London concert next month and an appearance at a contemporary music festival somewhere up north."

"He seems to be doing well."

"Yes, I gather there's a new CD out in the autumn."

How well informed you were, Carmen, my love, Christopher reflects. How many facts you let me have, and with such studied casualness.

"I was wondering whether we should have a party."

"Sounds a good idea. Where?"

"Whitfield Street."

"Won't it be a bit crowded and sweaty at this time of year?"

"I wasn't thinking of having it inside."

"What? In the street?"

"No, I have a better idea. The flat roof on the storeroom behind the shop at the back has just been resurfaced. I was thinking of organising some flower tubs and turning it into a roof garden. We'd have to share that with Dave but he spends most weekends in Somerset anyway."

"Excellent!"

"We can rig up some lights, borrow some chairs, set up a barbecue."

"We'll have to move quickly before the end of the summer."

"I thought of the last week in July."

"Before everyone flees to Tuscany."

"It's a bit late but I've only just had the idea."

She looked across at him with her eyes full of pleasure at the prospect of their throwing themselves into something new. Something which united them both. It would symbolise their new start, their revived togetherness. Yes, yes, too neat, an idea too obviously riding for a fall, but on that evening in Fitzrovia, as they waved the empty wine bottle at the waiter, gesticulating for more through the plate glass of the taverna window, it seemed just the thing. Christopher took Carmen's hands – more beautiful to him than the marble perfection of Alice's much-photographed pair of jewel-props – and held them in his. He lifted them to his lips and she gladly held them up to him as if they were yet another joyful gift, a present of herself.

I kissed your hands, Carmen, because I felt at that moment that we were free again, riding out on the skimming yacht of our love, swept by the co-operative elements, over the breaking waves.

How I mock myself now. How my lips curve into the repellent sneer of the cynic who has foreseen all, who is incapable thereafter of being deceived. But then – and was it worth it for such a moment, whatever the price subsequently exacted? – I could have believed in any proposition the world cared to put. I believed in you, Carmen. Never forget that. I believed in you.

Jimmy met Alice in Paris where he had been taking part in an international Webern festival. Carmen found this out and he found her anger piquant. He did not consider himself to be the sort of loathsome beast who enjoys playing with women's affections, setting one mistress against another, standing back to observe the reactions, the catfight, but, given Carmen's instinctive aggression, her readiness to judge and condemn her male partners, he smiled at her vivid self-righteousness. As it happened, his meeting with Alice was an innocent encounter with an old friend. It was malicious of him, he admitted, to allow another inference to be taken, to fail to quash it.

They met in a small restaurant of her choosing in Saint-Germain-des-Prés. She was in reflective, elegaic, mood which he took to be the result of her decision, finally, to quit her trade. Moving those beautiful hands expressively above the cloth to emphasise her points, Jimmy had never seen her so entrancing, so luminous.

"This is the part of Paris I first knew as a young model. I had a tiny garçonnière under the tiles at the top of a tall building and I was out every night, returning only to sleep. I can't think how I kept up the pace. It was extraordinary, you know, the sheer speed of that life. Though I suppose, compared with today's supermodels, I led a much less raunchy life. Apart from the endless Martinis, I didn't do drugs or anything like that, though others did."

"What about life's other pleasures?"

Alice smiled sweetly.

"Oh, well, it was Paris, after all."

"How did you get into all that?"

"Oh the usual chain of accidents. It was a friend of my uncle's who made the first introduction. He was at a fairly senior level in the rag trade and knew lots of people. Everyone knows I had the looks for it. But looks date, and by the Eighties I was beginning to seem not exactly the thing. It was a canny move on the part of my agent to start targeting the market for traditional high chic. I don't think I would have held my own against the eighties crowd. I'm not Kate Moss, am I?"

"Alice you are not, as a grateful world can attest."

"I don't mind those girls. Under the sham accents and high-class slumming I can see myself. I was hardly less ruthless or manipulative. It was a form of defence by attack. You were so much at other people's mercy you had to fight the few battles you could win for yourself. But taking the direction I did, I added another ten years to my career."

"And now you are putting it behind you. Are you relieved?"

"I think I am. I'll always miss aspects of it. There's a special kind of excitement that's simply unrepeatable. But I don't want to overstay my welcome."

"The book sounds interesting. Are you going to dish the dirt?"

"Not especially. I wanted to concentrate more on the inner story. Everyone thinks that one is just some feather-brained *midinette*."

"They'll buy it for that reason. They'll want the gossip."

"I don't say I'm going to produce a work of philosophy."

"No semiotics of fashion."

"No semiotics. But I'm interested in the dynamics of the business, how it finds people, transforms them, educates them in its values. I met Carmen in London and she was very encouraging."

"Well, that's her field isn't it, pop sociology."

"Thanks very much!"

"Sorry, I didn't mean it to come out like that. What I meant, I suppose, was that she knows how to balance the analysis, the politics even, with the necessary leavening of juicy bits. Talking of which, is James Hermann, the concert pianist, going to figure in this tale?"

"Do you think he should?"

"Well, it would all be a bit old hat wouldn't it?"

"Darling, I *am* ancient, I was born in the 1950s. Most of my material will be ancient history to the fashion and magazine editors who all seem to be still in their teens."

"The 1950s. I love that vagueness. It could be significant to which end of the decade you refer."

"You'll just have to guess."

"If I had improper designs I would make some smoochy remark about it being no earlier than 1959."

"Instead you suspect, brutally, that it's closer to the other pole. You definitely don't have designs on me."

"Do you regret that?"

"Jimmy, I always let the good times take care of themselves. That was always my way. Regrets take up too much time and energy."

"So they were good times?"

"Of course. But we've both moved on. Tell me about Carmen."

"What is there to tell?"

"Oh come on, I told you we saw each other last month in London."

"Ah, girl talk."

"Something like that. I didn't get a blow by blow account if that's what you're thinking. But enough hints were dropped. She's been having difficulties with Christopher."

"The demon builder."

"They're such a pair of yuppies."

"I haven't heard that word in ages. Is it still current?"

"I'm too lazy to find out what the updated term is. But you know what I mean. They're always trying to make an impression, always trying to spend their way into people's hearts."

"Looking at the prices on this menu I was rather hoping that you might be on a similar tack."

"Oh, don't worry, I'll put this on exes. A business meeting."

"So what did you pick up from Carmen?"

"Only that she was unsettled and..."

"Playing the field."

"If you like. I've known Carmen for ages. She chose me as one of her first profile subjects – I was a 'role model' for the teen mags she was writing for just then – and we somehow hit it off. Because I'm always jetting around the world we don't get the chance to meet very often but every now and again we touch base. She's one of those people whom success has not been good for. I was cynical, I suppose. I let the good times wash over me. I partied. I ate at Brasserie Lipp. I developed a taste for the good things. I even hung around the fringes of an intellectual set. Deconstructionists I think they called themselves though I never got as a far as working out what that was. They dressed well, I have to say."

"I thought you were born to it, that famous elegance."

"Oh, Christ, no. We're all frauds in this business, darling. My parents ran a corner shop in Basildon. But the difference between me and Carmen is that I loved the self-invention, the sheer extent of the deception. And, after other people came to believe it, I believed it myself. Nowadays I couldn't rewind the tape. I've forgotten all the details of my origins. I am what I am this morning."

"That certainly isn't Carmen."

"It certainly isn't. She's hung up on her background."

"I know. We've argued about that."

"I tell her that it's foreground that matters. Shake off the dead weight of the past."

"Which, in effect – in the actual day to day run of her life – is what she's done."

"I know, it's all in the mind."

"I get it in the neck, of course. Jimmy the urbane toff. Who doesn't understand."

"The fact is you do understand. It's just that you aren't prepared to indulge her."

"Coming back to what you said about success not being good for her. What did you mean exactly?"

"She can't seem to handle it in the way that it ought to be handled – with both hands outstretched and begging for more. It doesn't last so you should bank it up, make the most of it while you can. But she's always at odds with it. I don't know why."

"The usual suspects. Guilt. Puritanism. The English class-fetish."

"Something like that. I think she quarrels with Christopher about it. Her discontent is dumped on him. I wonder if she wouldn't have been happier in some more modest way of life, back in the provinces, living in a calmer atmosphere."

"There's not much likelihood of that. She's like a junkie. She can't shake off the addiction to work, her restlessness and febrile energy. She has a terror of standing still and contemplating her own thoughts."

"I'm glad you're not like that, Jimmy. The world needs more people like you. Oases of calm."

The long wait for the main course was over. Unobtrusively, Jimmy's duck and Alice's wafer-thin lamb were spooned from silver salvers, their glasses topped up. It is strange, he found himself thinking, how forgetful we can be of sexual passion. How calmly we can sit and talk to the person we have known through intimate physical encounter. His affair with Alice had lasted, intermittent as it was, for nearly four years. Yet it was now quite over and unthinkable that they should ever breathe on its embers. He admired her nonetheless. He thought she had made light of the need that drove her to her self-inventions, of the difficulty of her beginnings. But then her beauty had been a natural gift that others envied and which opened doors. All she needed to do was to be its good steward. Her ease with herself was rooted in the knowledge that she had lived in the only way possible. She had discovered the law of her own nature and had allowed it scope. She had put no obstacles in its way. She had allowed none of its fruits to wither on the vine. Carmen had not been so lucky. With equal gifts she had not been able to match her talent to her sense of herself. Goaded by a profound unease, she had bumped and grated against the conditions life had offered her. She was condemned, it seemed, to a life of perpetual discontent.

Opportunistically, it seemed to Jimmy, her various lovers had taken advantage of this – and in what way was he different? They had been there when she had sought to fling herself against them, to whirl away from the situation that was vexing her. A new relationship, with its incipient excitements and diversions, harnessed her prodigal energies and sent her forward. They had known – he had known – the extraordinary experience of being loved by Carmen, the way she could give with such generosity of spirit in spite of her love of contention and conflict. No one who had shared Carmen's life would ever speak of her without acknowledging this. With Christopher, it seemed, she had found a more permanent relationship, an equipoise. Jimmy found himself hoping (hypocrite that he must seem) that they would find themselves again.

After lunch he bade farewell to Alice, took her hands in his and kissed them in a form of ritual obeisance which she had come to take for granted as the world's gift to her. He left her walking in the direction of the Metro while he set off in the opposite direction, towards the river. Summer tourists had thickened the usual crowds on the *quais*. The traffic seemed louder, his need for some reflective silence greater as he crossed the Seine. He walked on, towards the gardens of the Grand Palais where he sat on a bench for what seemed a very long time. Then he recalled an occasion with Alice, when they had found a little shop in a nearby arcade. He sprang to his feet and soon found that it was still there, selling musical boxes with a variety of tunes, traditional and contemporary. Thinking to play a joke on Carmen he bought a small wooden box which, opening, played the *Internationale*. He had always been surprised that Carmen – though occasionally making those vaguely left-wing noises that well-off upwardly mobile people make at English dinner parties – seemed never to connect her social rage to any coherent politics. He had recently challenged her on this and her excuse was that "politics have been abolished" by the contemporary practitioners – dull and visionless as he was compelled to agree they were – and that nothing could be expected from that quarter. He was still unsatisfied at her readiness to acquiesce in this collapse of the responsible public sphere. With her experience and energy and disposition she should have been at the forefront of the battle to radicalise her crumbling, ancestor-worshipping, insular polity. But she had abandoned it – like so many of the best and brightest of her generation – to its somnolent decay. Jimmy knew that he was in a weak position for berating her. His rootless cosmopolitanism (he was on no voters' register) and his total commitment to his music made him an effete force in this important argument.

Jimmy stepped out onto the gravel walk of the Grand Palais and opened the lid of the box. Its tiny tune strained to make an impact in this large and open space. An elderly woman (he thought of the tutelary spirit of this place, Colette) pulled along by her white poodle, caught the outline of the tune as he passed. She smiled at him a knowing smile. An old Communist perhaps. Or merely a metropolitan cynic – tolerant and sardonic – amused at the silly foible of another passer-by. He snapped the lid shut and slipped it back into its presentation box. Time was passing and he was due to catch the late train back to London. He set off to his hotel at a brisk pace to collect his baggage, threading his way through the tourists who once again dominated every inch of pavement. Jimmy wondered how long it would be after he returned to London before he began to confront the question of whether he should contact Carmen again.

Carmen went back to Jimmy. She knew that she should not have gone back. It was the third time that she had done this to Christopher – for that is how she saw things now. Later, freed from the reasons that she was able to advance to herself at that time, she could see what the real nature of her actions was. It was clear to her that she had betrayed him. That is not a term she would once have used but now she had a decided preference for these old-fashioned but vigorous terms. Betrayal of trust, deceit, lies. Who knows, she laughed to herself, I may one day come to see myself as a wicked strumpet. Three times the cock crowed. Three times the choice was presented and the same option taken. Three times she allowed herself to do the wrong thing. In her earlier, libertarian, period such a construction would have seemed laughable. Bourgeois guilt, bourgeois moral-ity, bourgeois possessiveness. Capitalism's acquisitive, male-dominated, hierarchical ethic reaching into the bedroom itself. How cleverly they deconstructed all that, exposed its shyly covered limbs, mocking those who had not attained to the same degree of insight. It astonished her to think how confident they were that they knew all the answers. For now she knew one thing only, one big thing. She had lost the only man in her life who loved her without reserve or calculation. She could not even say that she lost him. She threw him away. Wilfully.

Perhaps it was Jimmy's naturally nomadic way of living. Perhaps it was his fondness for a stylish backdrop, but their affairs always seemed to be played out on a foreign stage. It helped Carmen to create a sense of distance. In his case it was perhaps a matter of avoiding embarrassments. It gave them the illusion of a newly stretched canvas on which they could begin to execute the work in progress.

What was that work?

It was – take for granted the mutual pleasure, the symbiotic motions of desire – a way of escape. More so for her than for him, she later became convinced. She was ostensibly in flight from a pack of unassuageable demons but in reality from herself only. He was someone who was easily bored because so many of his pleasures and satisfactions were so lightly won (a fact he contested hotly; it was the ground of many of their quarrels). A change of scene was tonic in itself for him. Carmen was the additional ingredient.

And so she joined him on a flight to the USA. He was taking part in another of his convocations of new music at the University of Virginia at Charlottesville. It was to be a mixture of performance and seminar, master-class and theory-session. Jimmy loved these events, the higher sort of adulation, the opportunities – which he genuinely seized, for he loved the work under examination – to explore the music, but also to display himself. Jimmy's vanity was real but engaging. He was not lordly or arrogant in person but as a performer he relished the public display, the small stratagems of the honoured virtuoso, the wooing and the foreplay with a rapt audience, the excited consummation. Carmen loved it too for she could see that this was his business, this was the core of his creative life, the thing that he did best and enjoyed doing best. It made her restless also for she knew that she did not fulfil her own desires with an equal passion. She had only success – which is a poor thing in comparison. Was this, for her, the secret of his attraction? Was she drawn, irresistibly, to this marvel of an individual who had found the Holy Grail, who was doing what he wanted to do and had, at the moment of intense performance, no wish to do any other thing? She was to become convinced that it was this aspect of Jimmy that beguiled her, troubled her, reproached her, held her fast in its fatal glamour.

This time, Christopher knew where she was going and with whom. The night before she left he was working late. They ate separately. They said little when he returned, dog-tired. There was no argument, no hostility, only a kind of sullen silence that could have been either resentful or resigned. When Carmen left at four to make her way to the airport he was asleep. She did not wake him, creeping away like the guilty thing she so palpably was. If she had thought more clearly about what she was doing, later reflection told her, she should have known what the likely outcome of all this would be. But at moments like these one does not think. That is rather the point of them.

Carmen had always loved the American South, having wandered in the past through Mississipi, Alabama, Louisiana and neighbouring states. She loved the slowness of the life, the lushness laced with the terrible memories of what human beings there have done to each other. Virginia seemed a part of this, to a lesser degree, but Charlottesville, with its lovely neo-classical Jeffersonian nonsense and Ivy League trappings, had its mind on other things. They spent a week there. Carmen listened to the concerts and attended a couple of lectures but was repelled by the jargon-ridden thinness of the latter. She was treating the week in part as a rest cure and, instead of exploring her leafy surroundings, she would spend hours lying on the vast field of the motel's king-size bed, sleeping or reading, or reviewing her life. This last occupation was always unsatisfactory, for her excursions refused to travel on new tracks. They began from the same old starting-points and ended with the same conclusions. She could not seem to break out of the frame-work she had constructed around herself. It was meant to be a triumph, a happy vindication of the new century's values: the worship of success, enterprise, the culture of money. But it did not satisfy her. Politics were moribund – but had never been of any interest to her. They spoke a dead language of morality and responsibility and commitment which she believed had been rejected by the young people she wrote for. (It was a cardinal belief of her profession that its members knew what their readers wanted, that they could second-guess with certainty their inmost thoughts. They were of course wrong, but that is another story.) Consumerism was both political ideology and religion and seemed desired by the whole globe. Carmen was a votary. She worshipped money and goods with a passion second to none. But she was not happy.

One night Jimmy took her to a restaurant with a little garden behind it. They were grateful for the chance to eat outside, for the summer night was humid. At the end of the meal he brought out a small present for her. It was tightly-wrapped up in a box and turned out to be a musical box. She could see that it was not expensive and had been intended playfully. She lifted the lid and it began to play a tune she did not recognise. It reminded her of a pious object she had been given in her childhood by a sanctimonious aunt who had made a pilgrimage to Lourdes. As she recalled, it was a grey metal statuette of the Virgin, under whose pink naked feet on a rock, the workings of a musical box were concealed which played the hymn: *Ave Maria*. It played one of those laborious, plodding hymn tunes that she associated in her mind with summer Sundays and devout processions in which she would form part of the pretty phalanx of girls in white satin who strewed petals on the ground before the statue of the Madonna, borne high on the shoulders of doddering men as if it were a funeral bier.

"What do you think?" Jimmy asked her.

"It's nice but I'm afraid I don't recognise the tune."

"Really?"

"It doesn't sound like anything I'm going to hear in the course of this week."

"Quite. I don't think Varèse has reached the musical box industry yet. But I'm surprised you haven't heard it. *The Internationale.*"

"Oh, I've come across the name but I don't think I've ever heard the tune."

"We used to chant it on student demonstrations."

"I didn't think you were the marching type."

"Oh, that was in the Seventies. After which I reverted to type as the odious bourgeois. But with your passion for the folk memory of the working classes I'd have thought you would know it by heart: 'Arise ye starvelings from your slumber'."

"If that's a representative slice of the lyrics I don't think I've missed very much."

"You haven't. The Red Flag is even worse. All that stuff about martyr's blood. The worst kind of sentimentality. And such plodding harmonies."

"So what's the significance – or should I be saying 'semiotics' – of this little box."

"Oh, I picked it up in Paris as a joke. I thought it might amuse you. But I can't get over the fact that you have never heard it."

"I was never into politics. My dad was in the Labour Party which was probably why I gave it a wide berth. I wasn't attracted by all those old men in cloth caps, who met in dingy rooms and went round 'knocking on doors'. I never understood the joy of interrupting people's evening meal and preaching at them."

"But I've lost count of the number of arguments we've had about your precious working class background. And all those attacks on my privileged version. I thought you would have been misty-eyed at the historical trappings of the great workers' struggle."

"I think that's all so outmoded. People aren't interested now in socialism. Even the word can hardly be pronounced without its sounding ridiculous. People want to party. To have a good time. They don't want to be made to feel guilty about pursuing money and success."

"Is that really true?"

"Oh, I don't know. I'm just talking for myself."

"But isn't that the problem. Everyone just talks for themselves now."

"We're not going to have one of those boring ethical discussions are we? Because, if we are I'm going back to the motel now."

"OK. Anyway, I'm not the right person to launch such an argument. I just hope that by ignoring it all there isn't a sudden and rather unpleasant interruption of the party."

The waiter appeared with some deliciously cool ices. It was now half past nine but the heat had only partly diminished. Carmen was annoyed with herself because, once again, she had (automatically, unthinkingly) taken a contrary position to Jimmy's. This seemed to be the pattern these days. She had always been quarrelsome but now it had become a kind of addiction, a need. You don't have to be a professional psychiatrist, she said to herself, to see where Carmen is coming from: the girl is frustrated and all this bolshieness is displacement activity. Yes, yes. I know all that. She knew it then as she sat with Jimmy in the steamy restaurant garden. As they delved with long spoons into the deep sundae glasses and smirked contentedly at each other, she knew that she had been behaving stupidly. That's not how she was meant to be. She was supposed to be cleverer than this. But occasionally that's how it is. We find ourselves

tenanted by someone else with a big mouth, crass and difficult, tactless and obstreperous. Patiently we wait for them
to go away but sometimes they are a long time going.

They went back to the motel in a softened mood. She
had recovered herself. Jimmy, as ever, was easy and forgiving. He was incapable of harbouring resentment. He was so
good, in fact, that it was provoking. His calm, accepting,
giving nature was in itself a rebuke that acted as a goad. Yes,
she could actually find herself hating him for his refusal to
descend to her level, to be as bad as she was.

She woke in the middle of the night and found her
thoughts turning to Christopher. This was unusual.
Generally a sort of automatic cut-out prevented her thinking of him when she found herself in such circumstances.
When she was betraying him. The air-conditioning was so
effective that she felt quite cold. She drew the sheet over
her nakedness. She looked at Jimmy's sleeping back. This
made her turn away abruptly. She was restless and uneasy.
It was as if she sensed that this was a turning point, that
perhaps this time she had gone too far, that Christopher
would not have her back. She saw her mobile phone on the
bedside table. The door of the bathroom was ajar and a soft
light from some source (perhaps the corridor or an outdoor
light) was coming in through a high window inside it. She
had only to slip out of bed and take the phone to the other
end of the enormous room and close the bathroom door
behind her. Seconds later she was treading stealthily along
the deep pile carpet so as not to disturb Jimmy.

Once she had closed the door she switched on the light.
She immediately found it too bright. The furtiveness of her
project seemed to require less brash illumination. She
lowered the drawbridge of the lavatory seat cover and sat
down to examine the dial of her phone. Christopher's was
the first name in the directory sequence (she had ensured

this by putting an 'A' arbitrarily before his name) and all she had to do was press the relevant button. She hesitated. What would she say? Actually, what time was it now in London? Wasn't there a five hour gap? Or was it six at this time of year? It was probably already morning. He would have left for work. And then he would return later to see the details of her missed call, to wonder what was up. She would have lost the advantage of surprise. But this was beside the point. She still did not know what she wanted to say. She did not know what she felt. She could identify only a vague sense of transgression, of having at last woken to the realisation of what she had done. Was she trying to seek his forgiveness? That wasn't really her. He wouldn't have appreciated that. Did she merely wish to tell the truth? That sounded better – but for the problem of identifying what the truth might be in this case. It wasn't a matter of straight report. It would require the awkward terms, the unforgiving vocabulary, the full resources of that blunt moral terminology she had found herself turning to increasingly in recent weeks. Somehow she wasn't ready for that. What she felt now was the need to speak to him in the old way: that carefree, laughing, facetious, playful, nonsensical fashion in which they had joshed each other at first, before the quarrels became more serious, before they turned from verbal play-acting to something more wounding.

There was a girl at school. Carmen racked her memory for the name. Theresa, she thought it was. They had once been friends in that intense but abruptly terminable way in which we keep our friends at that age. They went everywhere, did everything together, and then they fell out. Possibly Carmen had started to go out with a boy of whom poor Theresa was fond, whom she had marked out as hers. Carmen knew this but she did nothing to repel his (obviously clumsy) approaches. As it turned out he was no more interested in Carmen than he had been in Theresa and she was dropped within a week. But the damage had been done. Carmen could still hear her shrill voice echoing down the polished corridor that led from the assembly hall to the playground.

"You're a bitch, Carmen O'Hare. You're a bloody bitch."

She was right, poor little, tear-streaked, straggly-haired Theresa. I was a bitch, Carmen now told herself. A prize bitch. I didn't know then that I would make it into a career profile, a trademark. I know also that I was something else. In the right hands – and this was it, this was what I was groping towards – in Christopher's hands I was capable of becoming something else. He turned the key in the lock and the door fell open. I found that I could open out, that I could give. People saw those stagey quarrels and laughed. Sometimes they became alarmed. But they knew we were good for each other, that under the warm spring rain of Christopher's attention the bitch had flowered, had become, briefly, another kind of woman. I never liked to admit it. I wanted to be seen as a strong woman who didn't need a man to define herself against, to be grateful for. I could make my own way, elbow aside my own obstacles, make my own luck. But that was all bluster and now I was prostrate before the truth. I needed him but, because of what I had done, it was almost certainly too late.

Carmen looked down at the display. 'A CHRIS.' All she had to do was to press the little button. He would pick it up. She would say... what? She did not have the confidence to do this, to say what needed to be said. And there was something else. She could not face the idea of failure. That was another of her trademarks: Carmen did not fail. Carmen the success, crashing from one triumph to the next. Carmen the role model for the young journalists and would-be editors. She did not do failure. Nothing brought out her bitchiness more surely than the weepy female in the office who had been sacked, jilted, spiked. She was like a healthy person in a hospital ward, fearful that she might catch something. And failure was the ultimate curse, the plague that struck one down and left one to rot by the side of the road. She needed the steady adrenalin surge of success, the constant verification, the tacit applause. At this moment she could not face being repulsed by Christopher. She did not think that she could handle it.

Then there was a crash. The door flew open. The light blazed. She looked up, blinking like a frightened, hunted animal. Jimmy stood in the doorway, naked, rubbing his eyes, struggling to emerge from the blanket of sleep.

"Carmen, what's up? What time is it?"

He looked down and saw the phone. She found herself, like a guilty child caught in some minor misdemeanour, helpless under his peremptory gaze. She handed it to him as if had been the catapult whose stone had shattered the pane of glass in the conservatory. He took it from her. He noticed the name on the display and looked down at her on her ceramic throne.

"You didn't ring him?"

"No."

"Why don't you? Don't hold back on my account. I don't control you, Carmen."

"I... wasn't going to really. I just thought... I just wanted to..."

Jimmy was now on his knees. He took her hands and covered them with his own. He kissed her with great tenderness but when he looked afterwards into her eyes she could see in his own the unmistakeable signs of regret. He knew that whatever it was that they had enjoyed was now over. No rancour, no jealous spasm, no prospect of scenes. He lifted her up gently and led her back to bed. She lay against him there, reassured by his presence in spite of this knowledge that it would be their last night together. They both slept surprisingly soundly. The next morning they were preternaturally bright and solicitous, busying themselves with packing and making their farewells and arranging transport. They flew back that night, and when Jimmy left the Underground at Warren Street their parting was like that of two travellers who have casually and lightly met, who have exchanged addresses, but who do not expect to make use of them in the future.

When Carmen got back to Whitfield Street, Christopher was not there. He would almost certainly be out making an early start on his latest job. Tired and jet-lagged as she was, she started to pack. Leaving a note for Christopher, she gathered up her things and returned to her own flat, wanting only sleep and forgetfulness.

Christopher now began to think that he should have cancelled it. He was certainly in no party mood. That festive condition seemed, in fact, to be shared just now by everyone but him. But a certain native stubbornness made him want to persist. He had no taste for victim status. He did not one anyone to feel sorry for him. He decided to go ahead. And, when writing out the invitations, he resolved to leave nobody out. If embarrassments, awkwardnesses, resulted from his juxtapositions of guests, so be it. They had only themselves to blame.

A combination of instinct, justified suspicion, a brief newspaper report of a controversial statement on arts policy from a leading pianist attending a conference in Virginia, and a pained (but he hoped not malicious) informative phone call from a woman friend (yes, yes, but long ago) gave Christopher a sufficient outline of Carmen's movements. He was able to fill in the remaining details with a combination of fevered imagining, righteous contempt, and stabbing regret. He could not say whether he knew with certainty that it was over or whether he still hoped that they could crawl out from under this amatory wreckage intact, ready to give it one more try. These things are never cut and dried. His thoughts and feelings were confused.

About Jimmy he was less confused. He knew that one should not succumb to jealous rage, to wishing the wretched rival more than metaphoric harm. After all, he had not himself behaved in an exemplary fashion and this was a relationship founded on comfortably old-fashioned libertarian principles, an 'open' relationship being the arch term of art. Neither of them was meant to entertain for a moment the usual forms of jealousy or attempt any control of the other partner's sexual freedom. But that was the official ideology. Beneath it was written another script which specified the appropriate moves with greater precision, which set out what was really allowed and disallowed. He could never fail to see Jimmy as anything other than an opportunist, a serene predator who did not care for either of them but only for his own pleasure. He was a connoisseur, a sexual gourmet, a collector of beautiful women. His charms were obvious and of a kind that Christopher could never hope to emulate. They were the product of the culture that had made him, inescapably, what he was.

Christopher felt that his own country at the start of the new century had lost something of its intelligence and grace in the art of living, a coarse Anglo-Saxon streak (always present in the *rosbif* caricature of continental Europeans) coming too much to the fore and cross-breeding with the showy materialism that went under the general heading of 'style', and about which Carmen in her magazine pieces was such an expert pundit. Jimmy's manner spoke of something else, of another possibility, of a road not taken. Christopher also admired, without reserve, his dedication to his music, the skill of his interpretation, that special liquid grace of his playing, and the largeness of his aesthetic vision. Had Carmen's life not become intertwined with his, he should have been an unreserved admirer.

But he was not permitted to be so dispassionate in his assessment of Jimmy. No doubt his unhurried charm, the universal adulation, were temptations too strong for anyone to resist. Women were drawn to him for reasons so obvious as hardly to need stating. And why would he have wished to turn them away? His wandering lifestyle was not an encouragement to settled domesticity – even if his temperament had been disposed to it – and the intense but short-lived affair, the plucking of the most interesting and fragrant blooms, suited him admirably. Christopher was merely unlucky and found it hard to draw up a convincing indictment, however bitter (and coarse its expression) his resentment could be at times.

He was shocked, during a particularly vivid verbal skirmish with Carmen, to discover from her that Jimmy had dismissed him as indistinguishable from his clients, seeing him as one of those fast-living new vulgarians whose money was being scattered so conspicuously around the capital. Christopher was hurt by what struck him as its injustice (later, of course, he saw that his immersion in this world would naturally have led anyone to assume on his part an unalloyed endorsement of it). He was also hurt by its ingratitude. After all, he had been generous enough to applaud his talent, might he not have conceded that he too was a little different? But perhaps he was deceiving himself. Perhaps he was more enmeshed in its values than he cared to admit. Those unleashed energies, the sense of excitement, the heady atmosphere of change in the city had undoubtedly captivated him but he saw it as a more professional, a purer (the word, he concedes, may provoke a sneer but it catches something of how he saw his avocation) engagement with the task in hand. He did not nod his head to the page-turner at the keyboard of a concert grand but he made, he crafted, something with his imagination and his talent.

When Christopher spoke in this way Carmen would snort derisively. He retorted that her own gifts were hardly a vindication of her early promise, of the analytic philosopher that she was poised briefly to become in her early twenties. She came back with heavy fire and they locked themselves into one of their fiercely staged conflicts which resolved nothing, but which blazed magnificently.

He was out when she returned from the States. He had begun early on a new bistro in Lexington Street and came back to a scribbled note on the kitchen counter: "Back from US. Jet-lagged. Gone back to my place to sleep. Speak to you later." It was her usual minimalist style and left no clues. He was inclined to think it a front for some more permanent disengagement, whose terms would be confirmed later when they had found the opportunity to 'speak'. As he walked back to Whitfield Street the skies had begun to darken. A violent summer storm seemed imminent. From the sound of traffic as he passed along the narrow corridor, he realised that the window of the tiny room Carmen used for her writing when she was staying with him (she had always insisted on keeping her flat, it seemed to him, as a safety net) was open. Lightning flashed as he stepped into the room to secure the window. The unnatural, sharp, electric brightness showed, what he would have seen in any light, that her possessions had gone. Nothing was plugged in to the sockets. Her minimal office apparatus (bear mascot, mug of pens, several box files) had been hastily scooped up. He knew that if he went into the bedroom he would find the drawers and hangers empty of the few clothes she kept there. There was a brusque completeness about her withdrawal that was also utterly characteristic: conducted at a run, without regard to how it might affect anyone else.

Carmen, he muttered to himself, I have called you generous, which, when our love was at its most extreme pitch, you were. You would surrender, and evoke, everything. I have never felt more intensely alive than during those episodes (pitifully few in retrospect) when we could, like Donne's lovers, eclipse the world. But you could also be cruel, Carmen, with a harshness that seemed to hold no mercy to anyone, least of all yourself. I think, indeed, that at those moments, you were punishing yourself. The rest of us were merely collateral victims, of little account in the tally of war. Perhaps there was no other way. Perhaps this peremptory evacuation was the kindest way to do it, as if, in the nature of the case, there could be no more tender stratagem.

Christopher walked into the bedroom, hardly bothering to confirm the evidence which he had predicted of Carmen's retreat. The thunder cracked and rain slashed against the window panes. He secured another window. As he looked out he saw people running along the pavement, newspapers held above their heads as impromptu umbrellas. A couple in summer clothes – he in a T-shirt; she in a tiny white vest and calf-length slacks – scorned to run, laughing, holding each other, their hair plastered to their skulls, their clothing tightly clinging to their bodies, enjoying the shower, ecstatic at their freedom, their indifference to what mere weather could put in their path. The more provident citizens, huddled under tiny tote umbrellas, edged along the pavement, hugging the wall. Rain drummed on the silver metal tables outside the pub, filling abandoned glasses in an instant. Puddles swelled above drains which could not take more than a fraction of the floodwater. And then, as suddenly as it came, it was over. The sky became lighter. People emerged laughing from doorways, cafés, pub entrances, spreading out their palms for confirmation that the downpour had really stopped. Barmen followed, wiping the chairs with sponges, tipping water from glasses on to the pavement, coaxing the refugee drinkers back out into the street. A girl shrieked as a passing taxi showered her with water from a broad puddle. Two youths were poking the sagging canopy in front of a restaurant, hoping to spill its contents with a terrific splash, until a waiter emerged to chase them off.

And then he saw her, working her way along the street. No umbrella, but she had clearly seen out the storm under cover somewhere along her route. Craftily, he watched her from his position at the first floor window. The sky was clearing rapidly. A crack of blue appeared and even here, in the heart of the dirty, dusty, summer city, he could smell the brief, steaming freshness that was being prepared. Carmen walked towards him, towards a confrontation that he no longer feared. He moved back from the window and sat on the bed to await the sound of her key in the lock. When she chose to ring the bell he knew that it was all over.

She allowed herself to be kissed briefly on the cheek like someone being greeted by a barely known hostess on arrival at a party. Christopher stood back to let her pass. As she sat down on the sofa he looked at her as if she were a perfect stranger and he were wholly disconnected from her.

"Chris, we need to talk."

"I'm sure we do. How was Jimmy?"

"Chris, this isn't going to be made any easier by sarcasms. Let's try to keep it adult."

"Adult. That's an interesting term. I must note that one for future reference. And I apologise for the sarcasm. I'm merely a manual worker, a yuppy with a power drill, as the great concert artist would put it. I haven't the time to perfect a more studied utterance."

"Oh stop talking crap. I take it you know where I have been."

"And with whom."

"And with whom."

"Well, I am waiting to hear about this 'need', about what makes it imperative that we talk."

"Ease up, will you, Chris. This is hard enough."

"Oh yes, it's hard. It's very hard. You've no idea how

hard it is. I don't think you've even begun to contemplate how hard it is."

"OK. OK. I have hurt you. I have made a mistake. With Jimmy it's..."

"All over? Spare me."

"Well it is. It's over, it's played out."

Carmen paused. She had been wringing her hands tightly around the strap of her handbag, fighting, it seemed to him, for a way through this that did not take her usual course of a blazing row, the discharge of all batteries. That was not how she wanted it to be.

"I won't be seeing him again."

"Third time unlucky? I suppose I should be grateful that you have seen the light at last. Should I be grateful?"

And then a new sound in her voice, never heard before, a tone that seemed to come from somewhere at the farthest edge of desperation.

"Chris, I no longer care what you or I or anyone feels. I am tired. I am exhausted by all this. You don't need to be grateful. I don't need to get down on my knees and beg forgiveness. There's nothing left in these gestures. They solve nothing. I've spoiled everything we had. I don't know why I did it. But it's done. Last night I realised suddenly, as if a light had suddenly been switched on, how much you had meant to me and the enormity of what I had done. I haven't come to ask you to take me back. I realise that I have lost that chance. That it's too late."

"Yes, you're right about that. It's too late. Too late for both of us. Too late for any more talk."

She loosened her hold on the strap. There was a long silence while she struggled to resume. He decided that he could offer her no help. He hardly knew what to say himself. Words were useless but they were the only building block they possessed. She looked up at him, more anxious and vulnerable than he had ever seen her.

"It is too late isn't it?"

He got up and walked across to the window. The tables outside the pub had filled up again. Some late, strong sunshine was washing the street. The usual number of people was at large. He opened the window but when he looked out he felt as though he was gazing at the street scene through a thick pane of plate glass. His feelings were numbed. He felt a dead, heavy weight inside him.

"Yes, it's too late."

They were beyond tears. She stood up – bravely he wanted to say – as if it were time to go, as if nothing further could be said. But then she dropped down and threw her bag to one side.

"Chris, does it need to be like this? Can't we forget the mistakes we've both made."

"You think Joanna cancels out Jimmy? That it's a simple matter of arithmetic, of balancing out the misdemeanours on both sides?"

"Of course not. I'm the main sinner in all this. Of course I am. I've never tried to pretend any different. I suppose I'm saying that it doesn't have to be so... final."

Perhaps, he was to reflect later, that was the point at which he could have intervened. Changed our history, Carmen. Magnanimous Christopher stooping, with magnificent generosity of spirit, a Christ-like forgiveness, to take the poor sinner in his arms, to whisper the words of comfort and reassurance. To take her back. To erase all that ugly scrawl of error and bitter words and sly betrayal. I could have done it. I could have taken you back, Carmen, but I was – proud, was it? What made me stubborn? Perhaps it was simple weariness. I had had enough, Carmen. I could take no more. And this has been the consequence, to become, as I have said, your sad memorialist, nursing my regrets above this reach of the river, chasing the phantoms of new loves, calibrating at leisure the exact measure of my loss.

After this the conversation went downhill. They bitched and sniped – not as before as a sparky erotic preliminary or playful verbal diversion – but like an embittered married couple whose relationship died years before but who did not have the courage to break out of the compound of dull enmity in which they had had themselves confined. And then they ran out of steam, became subdued. Carmen got up to go and, in spite of the thickness of his anger and resentment, he could see how final this was, how absolute.

"Will you still come to the party?"

"I think not."

"Your friends will be there. There's no need for us to cut each other dead."

"Isn't there?"

"Didn't you say earlier that we should be adult? Isn't it a bit childish to be like this? Come to the party. Avoid me if you like but don't let this prevent you from being with other people you care about."

"I'll think about it. But I really must go."

Christopher held the door open with the professional disengagement of a commissionaire. Carmen passed through. He would see her only once again in his life. The sound of her feet on the stair echoed. Echoes still.

Jimmy regretted Charlottesville. He regretted persuading Carmen to join him. He told himself that he should have intuited that it would end the way it did. It was not so much that he felt remorse at the hurt done to Christopher. It was the fact that he had almost certainly damaged Carmen.

He was not accustomed to these sessions of self-flagellation. The Jesuits did not really succeed in implanting in him their long, tapering roots of Catholic guilt. He was not long enough in their hands to have remained anything other than a deep-dyed pagan hedonist. He would not say that pleasure was his goal for he did not think of life as a progression towards an end, a completion. He saw it as a journey made more interesting, rich, vitally alive by what happens along the way. Pleasure is by far the most interesting thing encountered – on that journey to nowhere in particular. Like music, it is itself. It is not any other thing. It is not justified by what it leads to – or away from. There, a nice piece of philosophy.

His readiness to accept part of the blame was rooted in his conviction that Carmen had, as a result of her involvement with him, become a casualty. He did not seduce her. She was a strong, intelligent woman, incapable of being made putty in anyone's hands. He did not think he had ever met a woman of such extraordinary resilience and self-dependence. She entered willingly (she may have initiated it; he never remembered the sequence of moves once they had been made) into their fitful attempts at an affair. She knew what she was doing, as they say in the advice columns of the newspapers. She also knew the reputation of her intermittent partner. No one was being taken advantage of in this business. Yet he could have exercised – what should he call it? – a little more vigilance. He could have seen, like an experienced nautical pilot, where the rocks ahead lay. Dazzled by her desirability and zest he let himself ignore the warning signs. Yes, he was culpable. And now she had paid a greater price than he.

They said little on the flight back from the States. He hated these night flights, penned in to seats where there is never enough space to stretch one's unnaturally long limbs. They made him long for the night deck of a boat, watching the clouds race, taking deep draughts of air, or even the rocking motion of a train, with its snapshots of ordinary human life by the way, shunting and shouting on the platforms as one cranes to read the station name. The youthful Jimmy would have been able to say what type of aeroplane this was but his adult version was as indifferent as he had become to the makes of automobile. All he remembered was that it was large enough to have a sort of central space around the toilet cubicles where one could linger briefly, stretch one's legs, feel the circulation flow. Carmen slept because she was tired but also, he felt certain, because it was a way of avoiding conversation with him. He lay awake trying to imagine what shape that conversation would have taken. Mutual recrimination, Jimmy lazily playing the role of complaisant punchbag? Violent altercation resulting in vexed shushing from drowsy passengers, stewards being called? Or sobbing regret of the self-indulgent it-was-all-my-fault kind? With these possibilities under review he was glad of the cloak of slumber. On the back of the seat in front of him there was a small screen which showed, for those weary of the in-flight movies, the plane's course across the pole. A white line crossed the mass of frozen ice, a process seemingly without end.

For someone who travelled so much he gave very little thought to the question of destinations. It was one of the routine bones which Carmen would seize when she was in need of an argument. She was angered by his lack of unease, the patent absence of any need to shore himself up, to place markers along the route. When he had been younger and had won, precociously, some international piano competitions (goaded as much by family expectations as by personal lust for glory) there had been a certain satisfaction which even then he rationalised as being no more than the necessary knowledge that he had won the respect of his peers. The tyro performer, actor, creator needs these tokens of endorsement which say: you are right to continue; we acknowledge that your talent justifies your continued ambition to see it realised to the full. But now, in what he was vain enough to resist admitting were his middle years, the need was no longer there. He sympathised to a degree with Carmen's plight which he saw as the penalty of the upwardly mobile – the need to prove oneself, to measure the distance one had come from those diminished, meagre beginnings. He had begun from a point, materially and culturally speaking, where she would have wished to arrive. His argument that this had no bearing on the present exercise of talent was one which she summarily rejected. He said she was peddling Puritan propaganda. He argued – in one of their rococo variations on a well-worn theme between them – that difficulties, obstacles in the path of genius, far from extracting heroic powers in response, could sometimes choke off and destroy a fragile but important talent, lay it waste with too much discouragement. She would rage at him when he spoke like this. He considered that she was not listening to what he said. In his view she was thinking only of herself and her personal need to triumph, to be seen to be the victor. He thought many of her triumphs hollow but he held his tongue. In her self-righteous reminders of the milestones she had passed, there was a lack of compassion for those who had not made a like journey, who had fallen by the wayside, which he found bitter and ruthless. But she would no doubt say that in this she was vindicated, that inequality exacts penalties, piles up a tally of damage. He judged it best to say nothing when the argument reached this stage.

Jimmy had no real taste for these gladiatorial encounters and many times found himself wondering about Christopher whose verbal tournaments with Carmen had become legendary. He seemed to Jimmy a peacable enough type, unusually sensitive and 'artistic' given his trade – though that observation no doubt confirmed the odious-ness of his upper-class assumptions about manual labour. Carmen rebuked him for making the assumption that Christopher shared the values of those retail entrepreneurs and flashy restaurateurs who were his clients and Jimmy didn't doubt she was right. What provoked her about him was his ineffable self-assurance (which, merely to provoke her further, he called the handicap of my birth) but Christopher, he judged, was more equally matched, more likely to avoid the provocations that had been installed in Jimmy as standard. Perhaps their arguments were of another kind, more in the nature of lover's tiffs than the ideological/sociological debates in which Carmen and he engaged.

When Jimmy broke in on her in the Charlottesville motel he was startled by the way she looked up at him in a kind of mute appeal. She was holding out her mobile phone on which Christopher's number was displayed. He could not adequately describe that look. It mixed bewilderment, fear, pain, desperation. In that instant he grasped how much she loved him and the knowledge shook him profoundly. He felt marginalised, elbowed aside. Look at Jimmy, he could hear them say, the smooth philanderer, the posh one they think they are drawn to. But in the end it's always the first one, the sturdily loyal partner, to whom they return when the tempting dalliance is over. He knew that he would almost certainly never evoke such a desperate love in anyone's heart and he felt sharply bereft, jealous of that look, that love. He was angry. He wanted to seize that phone and hurl it out of the window. He wanted to tell her that she was here with him, that this was what she had chosen. But that terrifying vulnerability she showed as she turned towards him deflected his rage. He took her in his arms and carried her back to bed, holding her for an age until he felt the regular breathing of sleep in the still body which lay against his own.

She did not go back to him. She cut off her relations with Jimmy. All he knew was that she had accepted the offer of some sort of media job in the States but she did not write to him. He realised that he hardly knew any of her friends. Christopher he still felt uncomfortable about approaching for self-evident reasons. This was not the first time that a woman had passed in and out of his life (and sometimes the speed of that passage had been like the blink of an eye) but it was the first time that he had felt so troubled, so full of unease. He wanted to know what had happened to her, where she had gone, whether she had healed the wound he had dealt her. Normally he was serenely callous about those with whom he had been involved. Often, it is the best strategy, for both parties. But this was a special case and he could not put her out of his mind. Equally, it was clear that extinguishing her memory was the only thing likely to cure him.

Shortly after this Jimmy was asked to record a new piano work by a young but rising composer. He had performed an earlier work of his (bravely billed as the

World Première when it was done in a small studio in Lambeth before a tiny audience consisting mainly of the composer's friends and family) and he was very keen on this new piece. He found its uncompromising intelligence and austere beauty entrancing. It was a profoundly difficult piece to play and, in that week of rehearsal and interaction with the anxious composer and the exacting recording engineers, he was grateful to be able to lose himself in the difficulty of the enterprise, erasing in this way the recent memory of Carmen.

One night, after a long session in the studio which was to result in the final recording being made the following morning, he returned to his apartment in Regent's Park to find amongst the fan of junk mail which he carried with a glass of wine to the sofa, an invitation to a party. To his surprise it was from Christopher and on the stiff green card he had scribbled a note: "It would really be very nice if you could come." Jimmy hesitated. He dismissed the idea that he was being set up, invited there to be mocked or abused for his trifling with Carmen (as it would be represented). But there were other reasons to hesitate. He feared that Christopher might be concerned to implicate him in his predicament – in the way that the bereaved mournfully pool their shared versions of loss. Jimmy had always shrunk from the horrors of male bonding (his education having made of him a stoic in that regard) and he had rather face his feelings about Carmen on his own. Furthermore, it was quite likely that he would not know any of the other guests and that – here, once again, he must risk sounding snobbish – they would not be the sort of people from whose company he would derive much pleasure in the course of an evening. But there was a quality of sincerity in Christopher's appeal. He felt sure that Carmen could not possibly be amongst the invitees. He assumed that she would have exercised the freedom of the freelance to fly to the States almost immediately and besides, the presence of either Christopher or himself would have been sufficient to persuade her to decline an invitation.

Jimmy put down the other letters (unsolicited appeals from his bank and other banks to borrow money he did not wish to borrow) and sipped his wine. The invitation card had been wittily designed as a cartoon which represented a fenced-in roof garden where crowds of people (some of whom he suspected were recognisable caricatures to the other guests) were partying. As it happened there was a party being thrown by his composer the same evening but he could quite easily move from one to the other event. Given the dullness of the composer – in such contrast to the fascination of his music – he would be glad of the excuse to leave early. Benjamin was a lank, earnest, young man with a shaven head and a habit of wearing a sort of oriental loose pyjama suit of wrinkled grey linen. He treated Jimmy with great reverence, probably because he envied, and hoped to acquire, the celebrity he enjoyed, and always approached him with a solemn intensity and a limply outstretched hand. Jimmy could quite imagine finding an hour or two with Benjamin an adequate length of time on a Saturday night.

Nor, if he was honest, had Jimmy allowed himself to over-look the fact that at parties one is always exposed to the possibility of meeting someone interesting or attractive, something not to be dismissed lightly when one is, as he now was, formally unattached.

~ THREE ~

If one is an impulsive character – which Carmen was generally taken to be – one does not resolve on a course of action by some process of moral mathematics, balancing the pros and cons, and following the findings of the scale. But at some level a reconciliation of possibilities must surely take place – even if the decisive response appears instinctive and thoughtless. Having cut free from two men with whom, at various times she had been happy, but who now represented the source of her current misery, Carmen's decision should have been to avoid any further contact. That should have been obvious. But in spite of this she chose to accept Christopher's invitation and to go to the party. She had not, however, expected to see Jimmy. Perhaps she chose to go – this was her later rationalisation of the intuitive urge – because she wanted to demonstrate (to herself if to no other) that she was free of them, that she had regained her liberty of action. She had no intention of being cowed, of keeping out of sight, of steering clear. She would act in exactly the way she pleased.

Christopher, as was to be expected, had excelled his own high standards of imaginative design, his feel for urban theatre. What had once been a flat, puddled roof on a dull annexe behind a building in an inner London street was transformed. Around the rim of the roof he had erected ultramarine panels to enclose the space. At each corner were four spotlights, each with a different coloured bulb, the combined effect of which was to wash the roof space with a dynamic mix of colour. In the centre of the arena four trestle tables were arranged to form a large 'X'. On the tables were set dishes of food, and the apparatus of the bar. One entered through a small door cut into the large double gates of the delivery yard (tickets taken by Tim, one of Christopher's joinery assistants who had been instructed to be vigilant against possible gatecrashers attracted by the lights and music) passing a parked yellow JCB whose scoop had been raised to the level of the roof and draped with a bright red cloth. In this suspended mouth stood two musicians – a saxophonist and an electronic keyboard player, fed by a fat electric cable which dangled beneath them. Their notes poured out over the crowd on the roof a couple of feet below them. This striking mobile orchestra pit was the night's main talking point, especially when, during breaks, Tim climbed into the cockpit and lowered the digger's arm to allow the musicians to alight on the roof amid loud ironic cheers. Later, guests were given the story of how Christopher had negotiated long and hard at a neighbouring construction site to borrow the JCB, only succeeding when a bundle of used notes was produced – with a further deposit as surety.

As Carmen stepped through the narrow gap, handing her invitation to Tim, she was for the first time apprehensive. Perhaps it had been a mistake after all. Cutting loose, putting these people out of her life for ever, might have been the wiser course. But it was too late as she climbed up the angled wooden steps (bolted to the side of the roof for the evening) to the party arena. She immediately spotted a couple of people she knew, gestured to them, collected a drink, and went over. Pete was literary editor of one of the broadsheets for which she had done some work – but never for his pages, in spite of the increasing confluence of arts coverage and the sort of stylish trivia she pumped out. He was engaged with Kate (a deputy features editor who had commissioned pieces from Carmen) in a discussion about the sudden retirement of some BBC big cheese. She was not impressed by the departing mogul.

"The man was a complete wanker."

"I couldn't disagree more. He had an incredibly sophisticated feel for the younger audiences, especially that tricky 18-30 age group."

"I don't see what's 'tricky' about them at all. 'Utterly predictable' might be a better way of putting it. He simply gave an obviously cohesive and fashion-driven (which is to say conformist) group exactly what it wanted. That's sales tactics not creative programming. And I don't see what is 'sophisticated' about *Girls School*."

Kate had named one of the most popular programmes on the networks. *Girls School* followed the lives of six young women in an expensive boarding school in Hampshire. They shared a small dormitory which had been rigged up with constantly running cameras. The six had become the most talked about young women in Britain with their names and personalities introduced into the comment pages, editorials and political analyses of the serious broadsheet newspapers as well as filling an unprecedented number of column inches each day in the tabloids. Most notorious of all was 'Sexy Sabina' whose impromptu removal of her T-shirt in one of the early episodes had driven the popular media into a frenzy of excitement. This week speculation was running high on whether Sabina was involved in a lesbian relationship with 'Posh Patsy', a keen netball player who had been seen in the last episode disappearing into the showers with Sabina. The latter's lewd smirk as she turned round to camera had been on the front page of most of this morning's newspapers. Apart from one or two disapproving opinion pieces by random pundits and a ratings-boosting attack on the morality of the programme makers by a Church of Scotland Minister, the broadcasts had been hugely popular. Pete was determined to defend the programme and the role of the senior executive who had commissioned it.

"Kate, I print a review of X's new volume of poems on the Saturday books page and it sells 50 more copies if it's lucky. This programme goes out and is watched by millions. You can't ignore figures like that."

"Why can't you ignore them? You could boost ratings still further by broadcasting non-stop live coverage from a Paris brothel. Where does it end?"

Carmen decided to break into the discussion.

"Kate's right. Once you're launched on the ratings game there's an irresistible logic. Irresistibly downwards."

"That's the typical response of the cultural élite."

"Thanks for the compliment."

"Be serious, Carmen. You people always think you know best, that you can second guess what people want."

"Oh, I think the producers of *Girls School* are much more adept at that."

"So what do you want? Come back, Lord Reith, all is forgiven? Let the people have what some repressed Calvinist with interesting private sexual tastes thinks is good for it?"

"Carmen! I've got it!" Kate interrupted. "*Lord Reith Uncovered*. Next season's ratings-buster."

"Very funny. But I still think you are patronising people."

"I wondered when that word was going to surface. The people doing the patronising are the people who think that all we want to see from our sitting room sofas is the fleeting glimpse of some teenage girl's bum. Who think that real scripted drama, challenging stuff, is too good for us."

Kate nodded slowly and drew deeply on her cigarette. She blew out a jet of smoke which drifted into the yellow glare from one of the corner spotlights. Tim had just brought up the scoop so that the musicians could scramble into it. They rose upwards slowly, then began to play again. Kate watched with wide eyes.

"The real point is that all three of us are churning out crap and we don't want to admit it."

"I don't know about you, Pete, but I'm glad to admit it. I've never tried to conceal my contempt for what I'm forced to do."

"And where, precisely, does that get you?"

"Nowhere, but at least it means I don't have to drape everything I do in sanctimonious bullshit. Actually, I think TV is a lost cause. They've blown it. And I worry that publishing will follow."

"On that note, I think I'll revisit the bar."

Watching Pete go, Kate sighed again and drew once more on her cigarette. Fixing her gaze briefly on a couple who were wrapped around each other in the blue light of the diagonally opposite spotlight, she turned inquisitively towards Carmen.

"I was surprised to see you here, Car."

"In some ways I am just as surprised to see myself here."

"Just wanted to have a last look around?"

"Maybe. If I've got to start again I might as well keep my social muscles in good shape."

"Musn't get flabby. Have you spotted anyone interesting?"

"Not in that sense. I don't think that's on the agenda tonight. What about yourself?"

"Oh, always ready to take an opportunity should it present itself. Ah, isn't that Jimmy arriving?"

"What?"

Carmen looked around in time to catch sight of Jimmy

stepping off the angled stairs on to the roof, like someone disembarking on a helipad. He always cut a dash. He knew how to arrive. Already people were moving towards him, disposing themselves around him, responding to his presence, taking up positions. Perhaps this was what differentiated them. Jimmy was a performer, with a performer's sense of how he looked, how the audience could be played, what moves at this time and in this place would work and which would be best held over for another occasion. The space was too small, the guests too carefully picked for anyone to lose themselves here. It was only a matter of time before Jimmy made his way to her. She knew he would be unruffled, calm and self-possessed, cool as a cucumber. Whether she could match his cool was quite another question. And then she felt a light touch on her shoulder.

Christopher handed her a plate of small spinach pies from which he had already helped himself.

"I'm glad you came, Car."

"I nearly didn't."

"I would have understood."

"Would you? I seem to have lost my capacity to do that, to understand people. Or perhaps it's a loss of faith. Faith in anyone's capacity to understand."

"Gloomy reflections. We're all meant to be partying."

"True. You've made it look very dramatic."

"Is it OK? Not too naff?"

"I wondered about the guys in the scoop but then I decided it was a stroke of genius."

"There wouldn't have been much room if they had set up on the roof itself."

He edged towards the tables and put down the plate then came back to her. She felt that he wanted to say something. She too wanted to say something but she had no idea what words would have come out if she had been able to do any more than make small talk about the quality of the food, the set-up. He was soon drawn away from her by the arrival of some new guests. She was shocked at how different he seemed to her already. During their brief conversation she felt she had been talking with complete detachment to someone who was indistinguishable from any of the other guests. As she watched him from a distance he seemed a little isolated in his pool of light. More alone than she had ever seen him. She wondered, idly, if any of these lively, laughing women had their eyes set on him. For his part, he seemed indifferent to that possibility.

Thinking she had better circulate, Carmen moved forwards, in the direction of the top of the stairs. Jimmy had passed across to the opposite corner of the roof. Just then Carl and Joanna arrived, looking a little uncertain, she clinging to him as if for security in an unsettling place. They were relieved to see her, for they would not have known many faces in this crowd. Carl kissed Carmen very formally on the cheek and Joanna suddenly squeezed her hand. There was something refreshingly innocent and unworldly about the two of them, set down in this group of far too clever, cynical, calculating people – of whom, naturally, she was a representative example. They talked about very little. She got them a drink and handed each a plate which they proceeded to fill assiduously, almost certainly grateful to have found something to do. Carmen guessed they would not stay long.

Stepping now from the stairs into the blue light was a new performer, gratefully acknowledging the silent applause of thrown glances. She moved towards Carmen with her arms extended. The latter greeted her with equal extravagance, hamming it up.

"Alice! I'd no idea you were coming."

"Neither had I, darling. Something came up and I flew

in this morning. Isn't this a gas? This is the work of...
Christopher?"

Carmen understood in an instant the meaning of Alice's
momentary hesitation. She was letting her know, in that
meaningful pause while she played with the idea of introducing a qualifier, a tag, that she knew that Christopher
needed a new designation. She wanted to whisper with an
answering facetious laugh: 'My ex.' But the term was so
excruciating she could never have used it, particuarly in the
presence of Alice, whose gift was to render everyone
around her a fraction more conscious of the need to be a
little less tolerant of the usual robust conversational crudi-
ties. But how did she know? Carmen guessed that
Christopher had spoken to her earlier in the day when she
phoned before leaving Paris or later from the airport. He
would have been brief and tactful, economically informative. This set her thinking. How many other people here
knew? How many were following this little amatory drama?
Had she become a spectacle? A source of amusement?

Alice draped Carmen in her benevolence. She was
sheathed from top to toe in a silver trouser-suit – no other
descriptor will serve, but it does not begin to do justice to
what she wore. This suit, because it was being worn by
Alice, flirted, on the right side of danger, with the tinsel
flashiness of Versace. To say that Alice was striking, that she
turned heads, is equivalent to saying that the raising of a
theatre curtain provokes a mood of anticipation, that water
flows inexorably downhill. One found oneself, in Alice's
presence, searching for the human flaw that would offset
the perfection of her body, her skin, her hair, her eyes, her
poise, her dress. She was too perfect to the inspecting eye.
One wanted the reassurance that she was also human,
which is to say imperfect. Perhaps it lay in her very
consciousness of her beauty. This could have issued in a

monstrous vanity, a coquettish playing with all those eyes on her. Instead, a glamour of intelligent irony shimmered over the surface of her performance (Alice was never off stage). In conversation with her, one sensed that she knew what was the real basis of her allure, its fragility, its subservience to the inevitable work of time. I am lucky, her manner said, and I am going to enjoy this while I can but it will end and I shall be ready for that moment also. I shall not be preparing a disappointment. She inhabited this beautiful casing with vigour and panache but she was undeceived. This gave a pleasant lightness to her manner. It was her special charm. And everyone was charmed by Alice. One should also mention *en passant* that she had a will of tensile steel.

"Carmen, I spoke, in the briefest terms, to Christopher this morning – about how things stand between you. I think he may have been surprised to see you here."

"Perhaps I should have stayed away. One never knows what is the right thing to do."

"You did the right thing. There's no point in going off in a sulk. These are your friends; you are entitled to be with them. You have lost a lover not the rest of your life. Do you want to talk about it?"

"No, I am trying to forget. It was mostly my fault."

"Nonsense. It's never one partner's fault. I'm not saying the responsibility is always evenly matched – it almost never is, in fact. But do yourself a favour and dump a little bit on the other guy. That's what they're there for."

"I'll try and take the advice. How are your memoirs going?"

"God, you make me sound like a retired colonel reliving his campaigns. Actually, it's the reason I'm here. To talk money. It's what it all boils down to in the end."

"I presume there'll be plenty of it."

"I guess so. When I told them about the diaries I had kept for the past twenty years I could see a few noughts being added. I didn't think too much about it at the time – and God knows how I found the time to keep them, given the whirl in which I lived – but I now realise they are pure dynamite. I met a lot of people, you see, in London, Paris, New York, Milan and so forth. And they were the sort who yield up the right material. Not just people in the trade but all the hangers-on. Politicians, film-stars, writers, acceptable crooks. The catwalk is like one of those strips hung up to catch flies. They can't keep away."

"Alice, the sales pitch has worked. I'll offer you a six figure advance."

She waved the idea away with a short laugh. Her life had been spent swimming gracefully in a tank of wealth and universal admiration. She hardly needed any more. World-weariness she didn't do but she was one of the less deceived, the people who know what isn't good for them but who have no intention of acting on the knowledge.

And then he arrived. His sharp white suit as he cut through the crowd made Carmen think, absurdly no doubt, of a schooner's hull slicing the waves. He stood between them, taking Alice's exquisite hand like a restorer of fragile ceramics who knows exactly where not to apply dangerous pressure. She allowed her hand to be kissed and withdrew it slowly. With the same suavity he nodded at Carmen, wisely avoiding any physical contact. She liked to think that she had a certain intuition about these things and she was convinced that they had not been – let us say, recently – lovers. So Alice was not to be the embarassment. That was left to Carmen. For his part, Jimmy was not someone to be embarassed or awkward in any situation. His preferred style was the easy and unfussed and he handled the situation with his customary expertise. None of this stopped her watching how he interacted with Alice. She noted the way in which – through a code of ironic smiles, inhaled breath, sweeping panoptic glances, movements of the lips – they spoke to each other without words. This was the freemasonry of the socially assured, those who have never dwelt at lower, more precarious, altitudes, and, far from sensing herself excluded, Carmen admired its subtle grace – and knew (in Alice's case at least) that it was a delicious hokum, the grocer's daughter from Basildon mimicking, improving upon, the *hauteur*, the finesse, of a European duchess. Their tacit conclusion was that this was not quite their natural milieu, though each of them knew about three or four people. Carmen wanted to leave them to each other, to slip quietly away, but felt trapped, her back against the ultramarine panel, her way forward blocked by the way the two of them had chosen to position themselves.

Then Carl and Joanna awkwardly breached that defence. They forced Alice and Jimmy apart (there was a moment too much delay, a moment of rudeness, before they were allowed through) then stepped forward with outstretched hands to announce that they were leaving and that they did not wish to do so until they had spoken to Carmen. They did not seem the same couple she had met that evening at the table outside the restaurant where Carl had been distant and abstracted, Joanna simperingly sweet. They seemed to have taken control of themselves, consciously projected themselves as a couple. Carmen felt slow on the uptake in this particular department but when she saw Joanna smooth her stomach with the palm of her hand she was finally prompted to congratulate her. Carl beamed in a way that nearly made her laugh, not one of her mocking laughs, but in an impulse of amusement at the way in which he so comfortably, so complacently acted his part. They now proved useful to Carmen as a stalking horse to get herself out of this corner. Once she had made her escape, Alice and Jimmy advanced towards another group. She then neatly left the loving couple and swam across to the opposite corner of the roof. There a group of media friends was sharing a bottle of something special which they had brought with them and had been too selfish to leave in the general pool.

Carmen kept going for another half hour and then she caught sight of Christopher. He was detached, having just dealt with some minor electrical problem raised by the band, and she decided that this was the right moment to approach him. He saw her coming and waved. When she saw that shy, delicate smile she recalled the young man on the hotel terrace towards whom she had responded with such unfeeling sharpness. She could not help the way she was (or so she habitually argued) but there were times when she could have wished for some greater measure of sweetness in her nature, some adeptness in the easier kinds of charm. It was fatally easy to play the role of hard bitch and it was one into which she slipped far too frequently. There had been good times, times when he had brought from her what she did not know was there, what he called her generosity. Carmen never understood this choice of term. She did not see herself as the embodiment of this virtue but she came to understand that he meant her passion, her energy, her intensity, her refusal to be indifferent (but also her indifference to what the world might think). It was this, he claimed, that liberated his own passions and intensities. Yes, there had been good times, and now they had come to an end. She did not know why. In these circumstances one never does. One simply bows to one's fate.

Carmen crossed towards him and touched him lightly on the arm.

"Chris, I must be going."

"I'm so glad you came. You saw everyone? Alice was Alice in spades, don't you think?"

"She always is. She never does things by halves."

"Carl and Joanna seem very happy."

"Yes, even I was touched."

Christopher laughed sardonically. Carmen struggled to say something. She wanted to leave with some suitable word but it was not proving easy. She thought that he saw this.

"So you're off to the States?"

"Monday morning. It's only a twelve month contract but who knows?"

"I nearly said let's keep in touch but that's fatuous isn't it?"

"I suppose it is... Chris, there's so much I want to say but I can't seem to express anything."

"That's OK. We both know what the words would say if they could come out but sometimes it's better to say nothing, to let go."

She touched his arm again. She turned away just as someone was coming up to him with another request and managed to get to the head of the steps before he could say anything more. Tim was at the bottom of the flight, sitting on two crates having a cigarette. He nodded at Carmen and opened the small door allowing her out into the street. It was nearly midnight, she supposed, and in spite of its being Saturday night there were few people about. She cut through to Tottenham Court Road, which was a little rowdier and noisier, and caught a night bus which was surprisingly full and jolly. Most people on the bus were drunk or coming home from having a good time and there was a sense of laughing camaraderie on the top deck.

It was just at this point, after all this time, after everything, that Carmen finally broke down and cried like a child. She was crying for Carmen. Carmen O'Hare, the bloody bitch who in spite of being so damned smart could not stop herself from throwing away the only chances of happiness that were ever tossed to her.

~ FOUR ~

Once more Christopher finds himself at the window, a sly voyeur. In his sights this morning is a family – what is the collective term? Might not such lexical games save him from this stultifying routine? – of Canada geese. They are pecking in the silvery grey mud, ugly at low tide. Their purposes are clear: to feed and forage, to survive. Might there not be something for him to learn here? There are several gulls on the peak of the bridge's high superstructure, crying into the emptiness of the morning. He who was so busy, so demonically active, has succumbed to a lethargy as solid as those banks of mud.

After a fall from a piece of unattended scaffolding, which prevented him from working at the same pace and therefore prevented him from working at all, for there was no work without frenzy in that line of business, he sold up his share in the Whitfield Street property (you may see an expensive furniture shop there today). Pocketing a staggeringly large sum and retired to this riverine perch, freed from economic necessity, to cogitate. His thoughts, he could report, had been prolific and without issue. He had been moving steadily into the deep, vegetable core of stasis. He was now a specialist in the pretexts for inaction. For every possibility, every sparky proposal, he loosed half a dozen counter-arguments, devastating in their power of negativity. He cancelled several projects before lunch and moved on to an afternoon of thwarted hypotheses.

His new obsession was the idea of travel. It is thought of as the universal panacea, the easy cure-all for the disease of ennui. It is compelling in its simplicity: look, move on, find a place to sleep and eat, move on again. It supplies the grounded and the baffled with the one thing needful: an onward drive, a proposal of motion, and escape from being here and now, a flight into the arms of the provisional and the unprescribed. Who was it spoke of 'the sins of settlement'? Let us stride manfully away from them in our hobnailed boots and bush-hat, finding purpose in locomotion, shriving in the swing of one's step. He had got out the maps and spread them in his window eyrie, tracing the course of a fat, looping river through the dripping green of a jungle, naming cities, deserts, mountain ranges, lakes. Smoking Mount Bromo at dawn, the sluggish Yangtse, the toot and churn of a paddle-steamer on the Missisippi, the turmoil of Calcutta, afternoons slumped on the slatted deck-bench of an Aegean steamer. Make no mistake, he insisted: these excite me. I am susceptible to their sweet carolling, their peremptory promise. But I remain here, becalmed, my face pressed against the cold glass of the window-pane. Inert.

The name of my condition is not ennui, Carmen. You come to me in my sleep, reminding me of our prodigal carelessness, our spendthrift love. For us there was no reckoning. We were above and beyond that. Foolish? Why, of course, what is authentic human life without folly? Wisdom is beyond us as a species. It remains a pretty conceit of philosophers or theologians, inaudible and antique, irrelevant to our whooping progress towards disaster. Disaster? Carmen, my love, my loss, do I exaggerate? Do I dramatise? I think not, for I am ruined. I am living in your wake. I am the blue smoke drifting under the window after the vehicle has sprinted. I am the remnant, the aftermath, the unpicked-up pieces, the flak, the outcome, the consequence, the by-product.

A barge is coming up the river. I transform its load of scrap into a royal progress. Scarlet and brass trumpets. Wigs. Ermine. Quilted gear. Strumming court musicians, yellow hose, curling pumps. Swift-flowing gaiety. I am diverted. I race at the speed of my imagination, the only asset I now possess, Carmen. Oh, and my memory. I am an accomplished backward voyager, a rememberer of lost time, a connoisseur of what has been. I reach back into the coffer of our mutual past, scooping up the riches stowed there, letting the handfuls trickle through my fingers, then I close the lid with a miserly thud, patting the brass-bound lid, snapping the key shut, tucking its cold, chain-hung steel into the flabby wallet of my midriff. This they cannot take away from us, Carmen. This they cannot cancel or annul. It has been, it has had its day. There is regret, certainly. But there is also a kind of validation which says: this once was, this is not imagined, it has its reality still.

Christopher no longer rails against Jimmy, the usurper, whose crown turned out to be made of paste. He was no more than a cipher, a minor catalyst in the process of the dissolution of that life with Carmen. He heard him today on the radio, playing Beethoven's bagatelles – a departure from his usual stamping ground among the avant-garde. He was beguiled by the music, made drowsy and delirious. From which it can be deduced that Christopher has not yielded to the banal invitations of nihilistic despair. He can be moved still. The world seduces him with its manifold tricks. He is not a candidate for the overdose, the slashed wrists in the warm bath, the last leap from the cast-iron parapet. He objects, partly on aesthetic grounds, to the vulgarity of suicide, but he deplores it also because there is still too much to which he is attached. Too much which he wishes to know. He claims the freedom to wreck his life. He has exercised that right with aplomb. But he does not wish to be the one to end it.

In their long talks, in their quarrels, Carmen told him much about himself. She was much pre-occupied by her own life story, her early sociological romance. But he said little about his own life. There always seemed, by contrast with the lifes of others, so little to say (the childhood in a council house in Northamptonshire, the scholarship to an old grammar school with red caps and a modicum of sexual irregularity, two dull and doting parents, his father a clerk in the municipal ratings office, his mother a doler-out and scooper-up of school dinners... he breaks off. The dullness is suffocating). Christopher had never been a navel-gazer, a seeker after that most banal form of knowledge: the syllabus of oneself. The world and other people and the things that they do have always seemed to him subjects of far greater interest than his own *curriculum vitae.*

This was one of the routine starting-points for their quarrels. His refusal to be sparked into excited fire by her class-grievance, the hardships she would inventory across the linen covers of costly restaurants, the rage against those who have had it easy – a condition which he always took to be the desired state of any intelligent human. Why does he say this now? Because he has left her with too little of himself, too little to remember him by. He wants to imagine her in her Manhattan loft – if that is where she has settled for the present like an edgy migrating bird – performing with him the same ritual recovery of memories, pleasures, moments. He asks himself what it was that drew the two of them together, what held them in that stormy, aerial mating. He seeks to isolate what it was, about him, that made the thing happen, sustained it. It is a question which, in the nature of things, he cannot answer. He cannot see himself as others see him. He cannot know what set them on this course. He can know only his own enchantment.

But perhaps she is silent. Perhaps she is not tormented. Almost certainly, she does not share his state of inactivity here. He sees her vividly combative in the gladiatorial circus of an open plan office, ripping into her new 'colleagues', driving onward, locking horns, engaging, tussling, notching up ephemeral triumphs and always seeking to conceal behind that furious energy her lack of belief in what she does, her sense that something better might have been allotted to her, were she able to discover what it was. There are mornings when he wants to tell her that he wakes with a brisk new purpose, when cheerful maxims bounce off the bright sunlit walls: make a fresh start, seize the day, shake yourself, get on with the rest of your life. Vigorously throwing aside the sheet, he races to the shower, cleanses himself, primps and prepares the battered envelope for its new adventure. Even the sound of water gushing into the kettle has a reverberance of expectancy, a prophetic music. Ice-cold milk, the crystal glass of freshly-squeezed juice, the reek of newly ground coffee beans, all endorse the belief that this is a day apart, a clearing of the ground for action and enterprise. A beginning. After these lively preparations there occurs a change of mood, a chastening. Objections arise. Difficulties queue in the antechamber, waiting for an audience. One has replaced the easy towelling bathroom robe with the uniform of the day. It is time to step out, to work one's way towards the High Street, acquire the newspaper, fill a plastic bag with miscellaneous provisions. Already dissipation is in train. The one purpose has been diverted by the many, resolution is weakened, the omens are not good. Returning to his waterside lair he drops the bag on the table, feels the glass walls of the cafetière to see if another cup can be risked, lets a glazed eye fall on the lurid headlines, senses, inexorably that the day, like a greased rope, is slipping through his hands at accelerating speed. He watches the craft, loosened from its moorings, drift helplessly out into the current.

And so, Carmen, he declares, I am back in my upper bow-window, surveying the river like a helmsman at his station on the poop. I sit at the light ash desk which I made with my own hands and presented to you, my love. I dream that you will come to retrieve it, just as, in a fairy tale, a shoe, a fragment of a sword blade, a gem, is produced, after many adventures, to validate a connection, to justify a claim. I shall not dispute your ownership. I shall ask for no proofs. You shall have it, Carmen, running your lovely hands again, as you did at first, across its smooth surface, trying the drawers, admiring the cut of its legs, announcing the great projects that would be accomplished by its agency. I remember one day coming to you as you worked. The screen of your portable computer was lit, papers were spread wide on this now denuded surface, you were intent on your world of words and no other world could gain entry, not even mine. I stood behind you, wanting to grasp your shoulders, wanting to break in on your consciousness, but I sensed the silent intensity of your task. I stood and watched for perhaps a minute then backed slowly out of the room. You never knew that I had been there. Sensing you.

This morning I trace a pattern on its surface with my finger. What I trace, Carmen, is a hieroglyph of emptiness, an alphabet of loss. I draw nothing in nothing, an extravagant loop of vacancy. I have lost you, my love. I have become the votary of your absence.

I get to my feet again. I feel the cold glass of the window pane against my cheek. It will come. It will come soon. The pointless, sentimental, self-indulgent salt bead that falls on the white gloss of the sill, drying quickly in the sun that now fills my lonely watch-tower.

A gull detaches itself from the tall superstructure at the south end of the bridge. It flies, slow and magnificent, across the whole field of my vision. It is graceful, beautiful.

But look, it is gone.